THE HALL of ART and PLEASURE

DARCY MONROE

Cover Designer: The Odd Seed
Editor and Interior Designer: Jovana Shirley,
Unforeseen Editing, www.unforeseenediting.com

ISBN-13: 979-8-9873822-1-9

1

ONE AND DONE

I was going to get turned away from the club.

   After this shitstorm of a day, the fact that the bouncer was taking his sweet time frowning at my fake ID shouldn't have been a surprise. I mean, what was one more embarrassment at this point?

To be fair, I looked nothing like the photo on my fake ID right now. The day I'd had it taken, I'd spent time contouring my makeup and caring for my curls—sure that whenever I ended up in a bar, I'd look similar. How wrong I'd been.

The bass boomed through the open doorway. A frigid wind tugged against my ratty T-shirt and jeans as I shifted from foot to foot in the crunchy snow. I shivered violently, but I didn't regret my outfit. I'd be damned if I was going to pay to check a coat.

I glared at the dark-haired barrier to the strip club. *Make a decision.* It wasn't like Cherries was my first choice of bar. My roommate, Bliss, had forced me to come out tonight.

After another long moment, the guy handed my ID back and marked my hand with a fluorescent stamp.

I glanced up at him in surprise.

A small dimple showed in his left cheek as his eyes met mine.

Damn, I needed to work on my poker face.

Have fun, he mouthed before I was jostled forward by the girl behind me.

On any other night, I'd spare a flirty smile for the cute bouncer with the stud earring, but tonight, I knew better. I looked like shit.

Okay, fine, that was dramatic. But I couldn't help feeling dirty after what happened today.

I finally slept with Brayan. Then he broke up with me.

Was I that bad at sex? Was it because I'd wanted him to wear a condom? I thought that was pretty standard. He was probably way more experienced than me. But how was I supposed to get experience without sleeping with someone?

My vision blurred with tears, and I blinked to get rid of them.

"Oh no, you don't." Bliss emerged from the crowd like my own avenging angel in a miniskirt and grabbed my hand. "You will not give that asshat one more second of your day. Four hours of crying is enough."

I stayed silent as she steered me toward the bar. My poor roomie had tried everything to comfort me after Brayan kicked me out of his car in the dorm parking lot, but all I wanted to do was lie in bed and sob. I'd still be there now if she hadn't guilted me into all of this. I couldn't think of a worse place to come, but I didn't want to tell her that. Why would I want to see a bunch of perfect women with no clothes on when my imperfect body was probably the reason Brayan had dumped me?

The line to the bar was three people deep, but Bliss jabbed a couple of girls with her bony elbows and managed to push us to the front. Normally, I'd have a problem with this brand of assertiveness, but I couldn't care about one more thing today. Instead, I wiped my watering eyes.

"Oh, honey. You can have a shot on me," one of the bartenders said, sliding a bottom-shelf vodka my way before mopping up a spill on the other side of the bar.

Bliss raised her eyebrows.

Great. I looked so bad that people felt sorry for me.

"I want to go home," I hissed.

"You want to take that shot," Bliss said.

"I want to take this shot and then go home," I amended.

"Then call an Uber."

I sighed. I'd never leave Bliss to drink alone in a strip club, and she knew it. And drunk was what she was going to be if she downed everything she was currently ordering.

Holy shit. We were going to need a tray for all that crap.

"Do the shot. They're going to bring the rest to our table," she yelled over the music pulsing through the speakers.

Our table? I scanned the massive crowd around us, feeling a little claustrophobic. There was no way we were getting a table in here.

I slammed the shot and immediately started coughing as the liquid burned my throat and tears rose to my eyes.

She didn't even give me time to recover. She grabbed my hand and pulled me through the people behind us at the bar until we broke free of the thickest part of the crowd.

"Why are there so many girls here?" I asked as she trotted toward a tiny, magically open table.

She didn't answer, just plopped me in the chair beside her and started fishing dollar bills out of her purse.

I sat back as a girl in the corner threw me a dirty look from her four-inch heels. Well then, why hadn't she taken the table? It wasn't like anyone had been sitting at it when we got here.

"He was a douchebag," Bliss said, misinterpreting my scowl. "I mean, who spells Brayan with two A's? And even if they do, no one wants to hear about how unique that is for twenty straight minutes! You should be grateful for what happened. Did you really want to date someone your roommate couldn't stand?" She winked at me, but there was an edge to her voice.

"I'm—"

She flipped back her platinum-blonde hair. "I don't want to hear about how you think you're bad at sex. We're in college, Kenz. When else are you supposed to learn? Some guys want to get in your pants and move on to the next girl. He picked the wrong bitch to mess with, though."

The last time she said something like that, she ended up stealing all the pens from the local bank branch. "Your overdraft fees are outrageous, and you deserve it!" hadn't gone over well when they caught her on camera.

"Don't do anything, Bliss. I'm serious." I'd never get another chance with him if Bliss got involved.

She smiled wickedly. "I don't know what you're talking about."

I stared at her.

"I have nothing planned … yet."

A server appeared with a tray full of beer and shots and plunked each of them on the table in front of us. Bliss parted with a few bills to tip her before she left.

"I'm not drinking all of this," I said, even as I reached for the first shot of what looked like tequila.

Bliss wasn't fooled. "Drink what you want. It's your pity party tonight. I can always order more."

I tipped the shot into my mouth and winced. I didn't cough this time, but it burned the whole way down.

I stared at the multicolored lights as they crisscrossed over the bodies that wriggled and thrusted to the heavy bass of a well-known song. Guys and girls threw back their heads and sang, their voices lost in the deafening music.

They looked happy.

Brayan and I had danced at a club. It was how we'd first met. I loved dancing. I didn't even need a drink to do it. He saw me with Bliss and a few other girls from my dorm and made a point to touch my shoulder when I was in the middle of screaming the lyrics to "Sweet Caroline."

"You're gorgeous!" he'd yelled into my ear.

I couldn't stop smiling the whole night. Not for one second.

I grabbed another shot from the center of the table and examined the clear liquid. So what if it made me sadder? At least if I got trashed, I wouldn't remember it. That was what was important. But I hated puking.

I traded the shot glass for a beer and took a sip of that instead. A dirtier song had taken the place of the crowd-pleaser, and the dancers thinned out, leaving only the drunkest girls and handsiest couples on the dance floor. I watched a redheaded guy sidle up behind a dark-skinned girl and grab her hips. She leaned her head back on his shoulder and continued dancing without even glancing at him. Maybe Brayan was in a club right now, telling someone else that she was gorgeous. Taking someone else out to Coney Island at three a.m. and asking what her major was.

I took another drink of beer.

"You okay?" Bliss said from across the table, distracted by the dim glow of her phone. Her thumbs flew over the screen, tapping out a text or a Snap or something.

"Yeah." *No. Why did you bring me here?*

She'd barely touched her beer, and she was still smiling at her phone, which was unlike her. Bliss was definitely an in-person flirt.

The music stopped.

Bliss looked up expectantly.

"What are you—"

"Ladies and gentlemen!" a deep-voiced MC announced. "Please clear the dance floor. Tonight is ladies' night here at Cherries. You know what that means!"

Bliss's Cheshire cat smile could be seen a mile away.

Ladies' night? Does that mean …

"I'm going to kill you," I hissed.

"What? It's a distraction. You need one."

What I needed was a pint of ice cream and fuzzy socks, not some guy shaking his junk in my face. Although … okay, she was right. If I'd stayed home, I would have continued to wallow until half past forever. My eyes already hurt from all the crying. I supposed … well, what could be the harm in watching the show? Tucking a dollar in a guy's G-string if I had to? We were at a dimly lit table, out of the way of the larger parties.

This might be okay.

"Stop thinking," she said, sliding a bunch of crinkled bills across the table. "Just enjoy."

Fine. Maybe I would.

The dance floor cleared quickly, girls squealing and pushing to get a good spot to better see the dancers. Those who had tables returned to their chairs and the drinks waiting for them.

The flashing lights changed to red and blue, and a siren blared from the speakers.

"I feel I should inform you folks that there's been a prison break nearby," the MC's voice said. "The inmate who escaped was charged with many crimes … of passion. So, remain vigilant and be on the lookout 'cause he's armed and dangerous."

Oh, gag me. I giggled. This was already ridiculous. The heat from all the people in here must be making me go a little crazy. Or maybe it was the alcohol.

The siren morphed into a staccato beat that thrummed through my body. I straightened the money in my hand. Brayan would never believe me if I told him I was at Cherries tonight.

Dry ice slid across the empty dance floor, surrounding a man who had snuck out from behind a heavy black curtain. His dark hair was buzzed in a close-cropped cut, and his body was covered neck to ankles in a bright orange jumpsuit. He played his part well, the perfect bad boy, exuding danger and sex with his hands on his hips as he gyrated across the floor. But buzzed heads and lewd gestures weren't my thing. Actually, I kind of thought he looked like a big Creamsicle. A sexy Creamsicle, but still.

When he began to tease the girls on the edge of the floor, my stomach clenched. *Shit.* We were near the floor, too.

He was halfway around the room, doing his sexy thrusting dance when he ripped his jumpsuit off. The squeals of the women were deafening when he exposed an orange G-string.

His dick dangled there, bobbing around behind the thin scrap of fabric. Like a Creamsicle.

Great. Now, I couldn't get it out of my head. I snorted, trying to cover my giggle with another drink of beer as he pumped his hips and thrust toward the closest girls.

Bliss rolled her eyes from across the table. "Just wait."

Whatever that meant. The warmth of the liquor and beer was reaching my cheeks now. It didn't feel horrible.

Keep the Creamsicles coming, I guess.

The stripper retreated to the center of the floor, where he did a rather impressive routine involving a backflip. Was a backflip in a G-string supposed to be sexy? When he made his last grand gesture—an exaggerated imitation of jerking off—the spotlight was over for him. He slipped into the crowd to give lap dances on the other side of the room.

It was all very amusing until he grabbed a girl's hand and ran it down his chiseled abs.

Just like Brayan had done with me.

"Come on, Mack. Touch me," he'd cooed, his breath hot against my neck as my hand skated across his flat stomach. Then later, his body arched against mine, his chest slick with sweat as he shuddered between my thighs. "Fuck yeah, you came."

Wasn't that the douchiest thing someone could possibly say? Because, like, (*a*) I hadn't come, and (*b*) why had he been sweating so much? We had only been in missionary for, like, four minutes.

Brayan wouldn't even make eye contact with me after that. Weeks of dating, of midnight adventures to Taco Bell, board games, borrowed hoodies, and all I'd gotten was, "It was fun, but …"

You know what? Fuck Brayan.

2

ARREST ME

The speakers crackled.

"He could make a nun sin. Am I right, ladies?" the MC joked.

Cheers erupted around us.

"And gentlemen!" a guy called out.

The MC laughed, and a bolt of recognition shot through me. I craned my neck to try to see through the crowd near the dance floor. Where was that guy set up? Maybe he was in one of my classes. Did they let sophomores MC for strip clubs?

"And gentlemen. My apologies," the MC corrected himself. "But I fear our inmate's days of freedom are numbered. Is that the fuzz I spy?"

Red and blue lights flashed, and a siren sounded again, but this time, it barely registered. The man who busted out from behind that black curtain was *hot*.

His arms were tightly wound ropes of muscle that dove under his short-sleeved blue uniform. And, whoa, that uniform. It curved and caved into every delicious-looking place on his body. My eyes traveled over his pecs, his abs, the visible V that led to a bulge in his pants.

If a facial expression could be classified as swagger, it would be his. He clicked his tongue and winked at the crowd. It was so cheesy.

And yet my body was responding.

Some part of me bought into this whole thing. It craved the type of man he portrayed—strong, confident, and very much an alpha.

As he made a show of searching for the escaped convict, a primal urge took hold of me. I wanted to be protected from everything that had happened with Brayan, from feeling sad and inadequate. Or maybe it was the alcohol hitting me, betraying me. How many shots had I done again?

I sat forward in my seat, gripping my cash.

Bliss chuckled, and I tried to swat her with my free hand from across the table.

"He's so your type, Kenz. See, this is why we're here!" she crowed.

I took another swig of beer.

The fake police officer strutted onto the floor. The booze and a lenient bouncer were why I was here, but she wasn't wrong. I preferred clean-cut guys.

When the music started, the cop turned to play to the crowd. The boom of the bass reverberated in my chest, a siren sounding every fourth beat. He was grinding his way to the front, and the crowd ate him up with their eyes.

How old was this man who felt so comfortable in the spotlight? He could have been twenty-one, or he could have been in his thirties or even forties.

All eyes in the room followed as his hips gyrated and his belt came off. He flicked his wrist, and his badge went sailing into the crowd. Cheering, a blonde to my left caught it and held it to her chest.

The stripper shucked his shirt, smirking. His muscles rippled as he flexed.

A heat spread through me, making my fingertips tingle. It was so dirty. Hadn't I just been under another man? But it also made me feel alive. I could chip a tooth on his collarbone.

He turned his back to the audience. His skin stretched over his back muscles under the hot lights of the stage. This man could probably bench me, and I was five foot ten.

I wanted to see this situation as the ridiculous scene that it was, but for some reason, it was hard to keep myself from imagining the way he'd make love to someone. No, not make love. *Fuck*. It would be hard and fast. Of that, I was certain. Were his hands calloused or smooth? Would our skin stick together as our bodies clashed, hips jutting forward, craving the release we'd pull from each other's bodies?

I mean, it was never going to happen, but still.

I drummed my fingers on the table in time to the music and downed the rest of my beer.

He pulled a baton from God knew where and twirled it a few times, smacking the palm of his hand with it. Girls all around me cheered. As inexperienced as I was, I knew some people were into that sort of thing. A man in charge in the bedroom, both physically and emotionally. I'd never thought of trying something like that, but I …

Something was wrong. There was a weird silence.

Did his song end? He hasn't even taken his pants off yet. What kind of stripper doesn't fully strip?

Bliss bounced happily in her seat.

Is this part of the show?

"Ladies and gentlemen, we have a special number for you tonight!" the MC boomed.

There must be a bachelorette party here. I swiveled my head, trying to scope out a sash or crown in the crowd.

"I'm going to need a round of applause for a girl whose non-boyfriend dismissed her today!"

"Aww," the girls around me cooed.

Jesus. That poor girl. How embarrass—wait, what?

My stomach dropped. The empty beer can fell out of my hands and rolled over the surface of the table.

"Mackenzie! We're about to make your night oh-so much better," the MC promised.

My eyes snapped to Bliss, who had her hand cupped over her mouth. Her eyes sparkled with mirth.

She wouldn't. She didn't.

She did.

"What the fuck?" I shouted at her. But I didn't have a chance to ream her before a slow, heavy beat started and the stripper began to strut our way.

"It will distract you!" she cried, but I could hear in her voice that she was second-guessing herself now.

Yeah, ya think? He had basically announced I was a loser who got dumped today! And now, they wanted me to go up there when I looked like this?

Oh my God, the messy bun. I was going to murder her. My face blazed, and I could only guess that everyone noticed with my damn pale skin.

When the stripper finally stopped in front of our table, I couldn't even look at him. He extended a strong, tanned arm toward me and waited.

"Take his hand!" Bliss squealed.

I shot her a death glare, then folded my arms in front of my chest as I stared at the man. Absolutely not. No matter how sexy he was, this was in public. This was humiliating.

"Take his hand! Take his hand! Take his hand!" The MC clapped his hands in time with his words.

The crowd picked up on it, and it became a deafening chant.

The stripper bit his lip, trying not to laugh. Was he supposed to do that? Wasn't that breaking character?

"Take his hand! Take his hand! Take his hand!" the drunken crowd yelled louder, and I let them. They didn't know me. This would have no effect.

Finally, the "police officer" spoke, his voice a medium tenor that was quiet enough for only me to hear. "Mackenzie."

I locked eyes with him. I didn't know if I wanted this or not. For a moment, I dropped my tough expression. I didn't want to be a part of this. It wasn't what I needed right now.

His mouth softened a bit, as did his tone. "Take my hand?"

The fingers I slipped into his weren't mine, I was sure. I would never have done such a thing.

He bent over the table where Bliss was waving a five-dollar bill in the air and trapped it between his teeth. Then he winked at the crowd as he backed up with me in tow, his body rolling and swaying as he did so. Catcalls followed him, and he slipped the money from his mouth to his hand.

I stumbled to the center of the stage with him.

From here, I could see the MC booth better, and I glared at the now very familiar announcer. Blond hair. Blue eyes. Baby face. It was Bliss's older brother, Trey. The pieces clicked together. He'd said he had a "sexy" new job last time he visited Bliss. I'd thought he was being sarcastic. What could be sexy when you had to work? Showed what I knew. It explained the reserved table, too.

"Come on, Kenzie. Be a little wild. Do a dance for us," Trey crooned.

The next time he needed help in Calculus, I was going to let him fail.

Trey gave me a once-over and said, "This is gonna be fun, my friends."

Apparently, that was the go-ahead because the stripper faced the crowd. "Are you enjoying the show, Mackenzie?" he asked loud enough for everyone to hear. He extended the five toward me.

It dangled in the air a moment before I realized I was supposed to take it. With a shaking hand, I snatched it from him.

"Put it in his pants!" Bliss yelled.

I was rooted to the spot, the weight of about a million eyes on me. If a lightning bolt miraculously came down through the building to destroy me, it would be quicker and much less painful than this moment.

What had I thought was going to happen when I chose to come up here? Cheeks hot with anger, I shoved the five in the waistband of his pants, near his hip—the only place that was even slightly appropriate. I made a conscious effort to look at him as little as possible as I did so.

The crowd booed. Not sexy enough. But they were the least of my worries.

Mr. Fake Cop pulled a pair of handcuffs from his back pocket.

His eyebrows rose, a clear challenge as he stared across the small space between us. Would I accept?

Trey heckled me again, correctly reading the hesitation in my expression from across the room. "Maybe she's been a bad girl. Maybe she needs someone to teach her a lesson. What do you think, Officer?" The asshole cocked his head to the side, a smile playing at the corner of his lips.

I stared back at him, folding my arms.

He shrugged in an exaggerated picture of innocence.

I'd deal with him later.

Returning my attention to the stripper, I swallowed hard.

The man's eyes followed the motion.

A hot energy pumped through me. My head swam a little. It had to be the booze.

He was still waiting for an answer. I needed to give him one, but I couldn't think with all these lights on me.

On the one hand, Brayan was like a big, gaping hole in my chest that I was scared would never ever close. I'd never felt more self-conscious in my life than I did when we were scrambling to put our clothes on. That awkward silence.

On the other hand, why not? I deserved a night. A night to do something a little wild, a little sexy. And what better night than when I kind of wanted to choose violence anyway?

The stripper's mouth relaxed a little, parting as his eyes lost some of their cockiness. As if he understood.

Okay? he mouthed at me, his back to the audience.

No one could see the way he'd changed from his "crowd" face of masculine confidence to the way he was acting now. He'd dropped the stripper act for a split second to ask me for real.

I glanced back at Bliss. She leaned back in her chair, smiling big, waiting for me to back down. Studious, safe Mackenzie. The girl who'd been dumb enough to fall for a fling.

You know what? Fuck it. I was gonna do this shit.

Adopting a facade of cool that I couldn't hope to pull off, I tilted my head toward the sexy policeman.

"Okay," I said, and the room exploded in cheers.

3

I WANT YOU TO HAVE SOMETHING

The stripper hustled me to the side of the room, right in front of a wall of mirrors. He pulled my wrists behind me to cuff me to a pole, which pushed my breasts out. He leered at me for the benefit of the crowd, one eyebrow raised.

It's an act, I told myself, trying to smile. *I'm wearing a baggy T-shirt, for Chrissake.*

He chuckled as he tugged on the cuffs, making a show out of how I was completely at his mercy. To the crowd, the fake cop drawled, "I think this little lady needs to be searched. What a pair of long, sinful legs." His fingers fluttered over the top of my thighs.

If I moved the smallest amount, his hands would be on them. Did he know? Could he tell how recently they'd been wrapped around another man?

When he made a show of pretending to kiss my neck, his hot breath was so close to my skin that I could swear it was almost real. The crowd roared as I jerked against the cuffs.

Their reaction was like a splash of cold water. This wasn't a thing happening in private. This was very, very public.

He backed off, an artist admiring his creation.

"She's too feisty to let loose," he told the crowd. "She might get violent."

Then he winked at me and grabbed the front of his pants. They gave at the seams, and he pulled them off in one powerful yank.

I gulped. His tightly toned thighs were bare to the audience, and now, he wore no more than a dark blue thong. The V that I'd seen a hint of before stretched down, leading down to an impressive bulge that strained against the fabric.

He moved behind me, dancing to a drugged beat that filtered through the speakers. He was so close that I breathed in his cologne. Sandalwood. I'd always been a sucker for a manly scent.

In the mirrored wall across from us, the reflection of him pressed against my back made my throat go dry. Despite the horrifying day that was today, my knees trembled when his warm body bucked softly against me. His eyes met mine in the mirror, and he gave one of those half-smiles only very hot guys could master.

I shivered as goosebumps spread over my arms. Smiles like that were dangerous.

When the lights switched over to a solid blue, I closed my eyes a beat too long. This elicited a throaty chuckle from him, which vibrated against my back. He knew what he was doing to me.

Fuck.

When the song ended, he freed my right hand.

I gazed up at him as he pulled me back out into the middle of the floor. Now, I'd return to my seat next to Bliss, half–turned on and half-dying of mortification. He'd finish by dancing on another girl's lap, just like the other stripper. I bit my lip, my stomach pooling with an uncomfortable heat at being so close to this man and his crazy-large … erm, bulge.

He stared at me with unfathomable brown eyes, so dark that they blended into the black of his pupils. With his head cocked to the side, it was almost like he was trying to decide what to do with me. I mean, what more *could* he do?

I smiled helplessly at him. This was his show.

He cleared his throat. "I think I might need to frisk this girl in private," he announced as he led me toward the curtain.

The crowd cheered as the spotlight left us. I almost believed he wanted more time with me, but then I remembered that this was how these shows worked. Still, I couldn't help but notice how warm his hand was as he held mine in the darkness.

When we were out of sight of the crowd, he fished out a key from a very private place and unlocked the handcuffs. Everyone else's attention was already pulled to the new performer on the stage—a muscular cowboy with assless chaps.

"Mackenzie," the fake cop murmured.

I rubbed my freed wrist, though it didn't exactly hurt.

"I want you to have something," he said in a half-whisper, his mouth millimeters from my ear.

"What?" I squeaked.

This wasn't part of the show. Was he interested in me? I couldn't handle that today.

His hand dipped into the front breast pocket of my T-shirt, and my nipples tightened in response as the hard points of a business card poked me through my shirt.

"You should go," he said, gently pushing me back out toward my table. Then he disappeared through a curtain that led backstage before I could ask what the hell was going on.

I sat in a daze through the rest of the strippers who strutted across the stage and did their thing, watching as Bliss threw herself into the performances, waving money at them until they came and danced for her.

"See? I toldja you needed this!" she jeered drunkenly at me.

I rolled my eyes, already forgiving her. This was who we were. She pushed me to do stuff, and I was the voice of reason. She was mothering me the only way she knew how.

Thankfully, it seemed that my moment in the spotlight was over.

And though I was dying—and I mean, *dying*—to look at the card in my pocket, I didn't want Bliss to know about it. She'd have an opinion, and I was already living in one of her harebrained schemes.

I played along and drank everything Bliss ordered for me and even let her pull me onto the dance floor when the show was over. I knotted my shirt under my breasts, and we got lost in the alternating neon lights, bumping and grinding to the beat and holding each other's bodies close. Sexual tension oozed from everyone around us. How many would go home tonight to husbands or boyfriends to finish themselves off? It was the ultimate tease.

Stop it, I told myself as I downed another shot. *Stop thinking about anything like that. Who cares if I'm alone? Just stop.*

And even though Bliss started pushing water into my hands at the bar instead of drinks, being as drunk as I was felt great. It was amazing. Nothing could touch me.

When we returned home, it was me supporting Bliss even though I'd probably had more to drink. I tucked her in her bed and uncapped a water bottle on her nightstand for later.

Only then did I think about the card in my front pocket again.

Bliss snorted as she turned over in bed, her eyeliner streaking down her face. She slept like the dead when she was wasted. But still …

I tiptoed to our shared bathroom and closed the door behind me. When it was locked, I reached into my pocket and unearthed the small card.

It was plain white, and the words on it were tiny, but since they were in a bold gold font, I managed to read them.

179 Maple Street
Tomorrow 10 p.m.
For Educational Purposes Only

I collapsed onto the toilet, fatigue and nausea flooding my body. What did that mean, educational purposes only? What exactly did a stripper know about my education? I was in college, for God's sake.

And I was so tired. I leaned my head on the wall.

And woke up that way the next morning.

"Ugh." I wiped crusted drool from the corner of my mouth and stretched.

Falling asleep in the bathroom? Not one of my finer moments. God, my head hurt.

It didn't help any when a series of desperate knocks banged against the door.

"I have to pee, or puke, or something!" Bliss whined.

I staggered out of the bathroom to the futon in the common room of our dorm and placed my head between my knees as Bliss ran into the bathroom, slamming the door.

Pieces of last night came back to me one by one. The bartender giving me a free shot. The way the cop's gaze had stripped me bare, though he had been the one basically naked.

And the card …

Oh shit. Where's the card?

I sat up in a rush and felt all around my body. It was gone! Wait, no. It was probably in the bathroom.

I dropped my head between my knees again to wait. Bliss noticed nothing when she was hungover, so there was little chance of her seeing or caring about the card. One time, she had gone to all her classes so hungover that she didn't notice a Cheerio hanging from her hair until six p.m.

When her feet finally appeared before me, I lifted my head again.

Bliss swayed before collapsing in the chair across from me. Her eyes fluttered shut.

I waited a minute, then reentered the bathroom and clicked the door shut as if I had all the time in the world.

Then the frantic search began. My hands flapped like demented hummingbirds over the dingy tiles. It wasn't on the counter or in the trash. Finally, my fingers brushed against flimsy cardboard as I searched behind the toilet.

Oh, thank God. I didn't want to take any chances with Bliss finding it before I figured out what it was for.

Brayan's toothbrush stared back at me from across the counter, perched close to mine in my rinsing cup. I surged to my feet, and with a shaking hand, I dropped it into the small trash can by the toilet.

I needed a distraction, pronto. Maybe the card was actually a good thing. Only one way to find out.

That morning, Bliss and I didn't step foot into the dining commons until well after ten, clad in plain crewneck sweatshirts and oversize sweatpants. With matching messy buns and bloodshot eyes, we weren't winning any fashion awards, but at least they were still serving breakfast. Pancakes were the best hangover cure.

My head throbbed as I grabbed some apple juice and loaded my plate with plain pancakes and syrup. Carbs be damned today. I'd go to the gym later.

When I sat at one of the long tables, I pushed my tray away for a moment. The smell was making me gag.

"Rough night?" a low voice asked.

I turned to see a blond guy with calm gray eyes staring at me.

I lifted my juice in cheers. "Yep."

He was completely alert, which meant he hadn't partied half as hard as us last night, and he looked all kinds of cute in his basketball shorts and school T-shirt.

He hesitated a moment, then slid his tray down toward me.

Yeah, this was not the time or place to encourage anyone. But wait. I squinted at him. Something was familiar about the curve of his jaw. That smile …

Though it was painful to think about anything right now, I knew this guy. Maybe. Kind of.

"Tristen," he said helpfully. "We live down the hall from each other."

"Oh yeah. Sorry," I said.

I'd seen him around. He was usually surrounded by a large group of guys, though. Where were they this morning?

He took a swig of orange juice as Bliss sat down across from me.

She pushed my tray back toward me.

I glanced at her plate. Bacon and sausage. Blech. How could she eat that after last night? My fingers went to my temples, trying to massage away the pain caused by the intense fluorescent lighting above us.

"Tristen, right?" Bliss said.

Of course she knew who the guy was.

He smiled at her. "Bliss, yeah?"

"Yeah. You sitting with us?"

"Obviously," I said dryly.

"Don't mind her. She's hungover." Bliss's tone was friendly. She wasn't doing that husky thing she did with most cute guys.

He chuckled. "I might've heard you come in last night."

"Jesus," I said, my face heating. I sawed at a rubbery pancake.

"We were so drunk!" Bliss giggled.

Okay, so maybe she was flirting. It was too early to be a wing-woman.

"Was there an occasion or just Friday fun?" Tristen asked, picking at his food.

Wasn't he hungry?

"Oh, there was definitely an occasion." She winked at him.

I set down my fork. "For fuck's sake."

"What?" she said innocently. "You were upset. I fixed it. With a strip club," she said suggestively to Tristen.

He choked on his water, and it splashed all over his T-shirt.

I handed him some napkins across the table.

"Thanks."

But Bliss wasn't done torturing me yet. "Kenzie was sad last night because Brayan, the douchebag, dumped her, and—"

"We both promised not to mention him again—"

"Except for right now."

I kicked her under the table.

"Ow, you little—"

"I think I get it," Tristen said. "It seems like you girls had fun." He winked at me.

I stared back at him a beat too long before I grabbed my tray and tossed my food into the trash. He was hot in a boy-next-door kind of way, but that was too much for a morning where I was hungover and still smarting over Brayan's complete lack of humanity. I needed a nap.

4

KIND OF WRECKED

I punched my pillow for the third time as sunlight poured through the dingy dorm window. It was too bright to nap. I rolled out of bed and pulled on some socks, eyeing my desk. Inside the middle drawer, the card was hidden safely under a pad of sticky notes.

Educational, it said. Wasn't that what college was all about?

I took it from its hiding place and stuck it in my messenger bag with my textbooks. Then I pulled on my boots for the short trek to the library. I needed to study for my Economics test on Monday. Brayan had always been so distracting, and now, I needed to reacquaint myself with material I should probably already know.

I found myself a quaint little study cove on the third floor of the library behind the stacks and set up camp, pulling out a bottle of water and a half-eaten granola bar to munch on. I hadn't changed out of my sweats, but it was college after all. We lived casual during the day, then turned it up a notch to get at each other when night fell.

I barely turned one page of the textbook before my head felt like it was going to crack open. I rummaged in my bag and found a bottle of ibuprofen, swallowing a couple of pills with the last gulp of water in my bottle.

I'd have to leave the library by eight if I wanted to change before going to this mystery house on Maple. I tapped my pen against the desk in an uneven rhythm.

What kind of stripper gave a random girl a business card? It was almost laughable.

Stop it. Focus on Economics.

I turned to chapter eleven. Dates. Statistics. They blurred together in front of me, policies blending into politicians as I crammed.

I must have drifted off because I jerked awake when someone nudged my shoe.

I blinked up at the guy from the cafeteria. Tristen.

"You alive?"

"Are you following me?" I barked back before I saw his name badge. *Ah fuck.* He worked here. "Sorry, that was rude."

"Yep." He folded his arms, the perfect picture of nonchalance.

I rubbed my hands over my face, trying to clear the fog from my brain. "Sorry."

"You said that. My shift is over in five. Do you need me to walk you back to the dorm? I'm not following you, but I'm pretty sure I know where you live, and you seem to be a little, um … tired."

I pulled my phone out of my pocket. Shit. I'd been here for hours. I barely had any time left before I needed to decide whether or not to follow the card's instructions, and I didn't even understand half of what I'd studied.

Tristen stared at me expectantly.

Oh yeah. Walking me home.

"Sure. Thanks. Sorry. I'm just—" I waved a hand at the open books in front of me.

He arched an eyebrow. "Professor Klein?"

"Yeah."

He leaned one arm on the side of a worn wooden bookshelf, his biceps straining under the fabric of his sweater. "The questions are all from the picture captions."

"Seriously?" That couldn't be right.

"Seriously. At least they have been the past two times."

"Oh my God, thank you." I pulled out my textbook again and began uncapping my highlighters.

"No problem. Meet me out front in ten?"

"Mmhmm," I mumbled around the pink highlighter in my mouth.

His face transformed into a smile, one of those megawatt, blinding types. His teeth were so white, so even. I blinked. Holy shit, he was more than boy-next-door cute. He was hot. How had I missed that? Maybe it was the fact that he'd changed clothes. God help me, but I was a fan of jeans and a well-fitted sweater. It wasn't overtly sexy, more like an academic smolder.

I ducked my head. How could I be attracted to someone so soon after Brayan? I should've put some real clothes on. And a bra. Yeah, that would have been helpful.

When his footsteps faded around the corner, I jumped into action like a woman possessed. I grabbed all my crap, shoving it back into my bag and racing to the nearest restroom.

When I looked in the mirror, I could've died. Half of my hair had escaped my bun and hung in frizzy curls around my face. Damn this dry weather! I knew better than to comb out my curls, so I settled for pulling my hands through them just enough to get them back into the stupid bun. I splashed cold water onto my face and pinched my cheeks to combat my paleness, but there was nothing I could do about the way I was dressed. I zipped my puffy coat over my sweatshirt. He'd already seen me anyway.

Minutes later, I pushed through the doors of the library to step into the brisk wind, rubbing my mittened hands together.

Tristen emerged seconds later, wearing a black peacoat and knit hat. His eyes scrunched in a cute way when he saw me.

Part of me swooned, but a smaller, smarter part said, *Didn't we just do this with Brayan?*

Without speaking, I turned toward our dorm. He fell into step beside me, both of us setting a brisk pace because of the cold.

"So, I've been nothing but bitchy to you, and I'm sorry," I said.

"Nah, you're fine." He blew out a breath, and we both watched as the steam melted back into the air. "We're in Econ together, you know."

Oh. That was how he'd known the test was for Klein. I probably hadn't come into contact with him since the lecture held at least a hundred people.

"I noticed you right away. You're kind of intense when you listen hard."

"Um …" *Was that a compliment or not?*

"So, that guy you were always with, was he the dude you were—"

We both hunched our shoulders against a sudden gust of wind.

"Yeah. That was Brayan."

"Ah."

A moment passed before I called it like it was. "Awkward."

"More like his loss."

I spared him a thin smile as we waited for a second for the *Walk* sign to light up at a street crossing.

"Why haven't I seen you in class?" I said more to myself than to him.

"I have a theory about that actually. Where people sit in lectures. It's nerdy, though."

One of the streetlights flickered above us. It was dark already, one of those clear winter nights where the moon was bright and the stars shone down, all still and solemn.

"I like nerdy," I said, hoping he didn't read too much into that.

"Yeah?"

The light finally changed. I shoved my hands in my coat as we walked on, my fluffy mittens barely fitting in the small pockets. "Let's hear it."

"This Brayan we don't speak of is a front-row kind of guy."

I rotated my shoulders, stiff from falling asleep in the stacks. "Which means?"

"Either he cares a lot about the class, or he wants people to notice him."

My face burned. Brayan never cared much about that class. Or any other class as far as I knew.

"And you …"

"Middle of the lecture hall before we dated. What does that make me?" I hugged myself. God, it was cold out.

"Well, you hold yourself accountable for going and staying. You wouldn't want to draw attention by showing up late or getting up during the lecture." He squinted at me before continuing, "And you care about the class, but you don't want to be noticed. You also don't wear a lot of makeup. I'm not sure I've even seen you with it on actually."

I wasn't going to stand here in the freezing cold and be insulted. I sidestepped him and started to speed-walk back to the dorm.

He made up the distance easily. "Not that you need it. And your hair is crazy cool, by the way."

More like a lot of work. "Thanks … I think."

"You're welcome." His voice was too nice. This whole thing was too nice.

"So, where do you sit then?"

"Uh …" He scratched the back of his neck. "I'm kind of a back-of-the-class guy. Sometimes I don't go, and sometimes I come in late. I don't want to be a jerk and disrupt class, so I slip into the back."

"Okay …" I tried not to think about how much my student loans were and what a massive waste of money that was.

"I know, I know. When I don't get the chapters, I show up. I just had Klein for Statistics, so I know the drill."

"I'm not judging."

He raised an eyebrow.

"Much," I conceded.

He chuckled, and when our dorm came into view, he nudged me with his shoulder. Like friends … or maybe something else.

I stopped walking.

He took a few steps forward before he realized I wasn't with him and turned back.

I drew in a deep breath. "I'm not going to phrase this right, so there's your disclaimer."

He smiled again, dazzling me.

"You can't do that," I said. "Stop it."

His smile dropped.

It was like kicking a puppy. Ugh, I was such an asshole.

"I'm—I'm kind of wrecked right now," I said. "So, if this is, like, you hitting on me or whatever, then I just can't." I wasn't even sure that was what was happening, but better safe than sorry. Brayan was still too fresh, and I couldn't make that mistake with another guy. It already hurt too much.

"Noted." He stared at me with an unfathomable expression on his face.

After a couple of seconds of continuing to walk together, I couldn't take it anymore.

"What?" My heart was pounding. It was about as bold as I'd ever been with someone, and that speech had been more for me than him. I needed to create space. I didn't want to jump into something with him right now, no matter how my traitorous body hummed to life when he was next to me.

"You just seem like a person I should know—all those highlighters, that cool, curly hair." He nudged me again.

I shoved him back, and we pushed through to the warmth of the dorm. I could use a friend even if his touch was full of sparks.

When we reached our hallway, he saluted me—a funny, mocking gesture.

I waved back as he entered his door first.

He was right. The whole conversation had been kind of nerdy. Dammit, I liked him.

When I closed the door to my dorm, Bliss was nowhere to be found, but that was nothing new.

I fished out the mysterious business card from my bag and plopped down on the futon. The gold letters shimmered up at me. *For Educational Purposes Only.*

I'd be crazy to go. Walking six blocks alone at night wasn't the smartest thing in the world, and it was freezing out. There could be an axe murderer at the address. Or a prank.

Pretty elaborate prank if there are business cards.

I'd never know if I didn't check it out. I rummaged around in my desk until I found my pepper spray and strapped it to my wrist.

Time to get educated.

5

PROPOSITIONED

The address led to a normal-looking red-bricked house, sandwiched between other similar homes on the block. One of those old places that professors owned or people who didn't mind the noise of living close to campus. A house with character. Maple was only one street over from the raucous parties of Greek Row.

I checked the numbers on the door against the numbers on the card one more time.

The January wind whipped through my coat. I couldn't stand here forever. Someone would see me. Was this the stripper's house? It couldn't be anything else. Maybe he wanted to teach me how to strip?

A chill ran over my arms that had nothing to do with the snow on the ground. That wouldn't be so bad. Maybe I'd feel sexier. It could help me forget Brayan.

Snow crunched under my boots as I climbed the steps to the door. I lifted the brass knocker and let it fall. Nothing happened.

Weak. No one would hear something so faint.

I noticed a doorbell to the side of the door and pressed it.

There was the audible click, but nothing else happened. I waited another second, then tried the door. It was unlocked.

"Hello?" I called as I pushed it open.

No one answered.

I tiptoed over the threshold and shut the door behind me even though this was turning into the beginning of every horror movie ever made.

"Hello? Should I come back later?"

I refused to believe that the person who had unlocked the door didn't want me here. Wouldn't they have ignored the doorbell or asked me to go away?

Damn my curiosity. This was definitely a bad idea.

My eyes drank in my surroundings as I searched for my host. Dark bricking in here, too. Thick curtains covering the windows, all deep maroon. The room was cavernous. Bigger than I'd thought it could be, considering its exterior. The soft glow of real candles lit the interior, standing in perfect little groups on gleaming tables around the perimeter of the room. Warm yellow light glowed from votives on the walls. I twirled, feeling like I'd stepped back through time. It was so classy.

Then I saw it.

A huge mural stretched above the door I'd stepped through. It wasn't by any artist I knew, but it wasn't like I was an expert. It arched over the door and flowed down the sides. And the scene it depicted … well, there wasn't really a word for it. Naked men and women adorned every surface of the wall, all engaged in some sort of debauchery. One couple was having sex doggy style, another man was sucking a woman's breast as she arched her back, a man was fingering a woman as she threw her head back in abandon.

I was enthralled. Who would paint something so graphic over the entryway to their house? It was so intricate and also very detailed, down to the veins in the throbbing erections of the men and the puckered nipples of the women. And the women were all different from each other. Dark skin, light skin, thin, tall, short. All seemed to be enjoying themselves quite a bit.

A small inscription above the doorknob read, *Oberres voluptatem.*

I pulled out my phone, my fingers shaking as I pressed translate on Google. It had to be Latin.

My heart stilled as I read the English version.

You're taking pleasure in it.

A gong sounded behind me, and I jumped about a foot in the air, the wind whooshing from my lungs in a surprised squeak as I whirled around.

Wait. Had that desk been there before? It stood in the corner, a single sheet of paper atop the polished surface with an ancient-looking solid wood chair opposite it. I walked over to see what the golden plaque in the center said.

The Contract

Contract? The chair scraped loudly against the floor as I pulled it out to sit. My name on the top of the paper immediately caught my eye.

> *I, Mackenzie Whitman, am here of my own volition. I understand I may leave at any time. If I choose to leave, however, I accept that I may never return.*

I agree to undergo a sexual awakening no longer or shorter than the time frame of one week and one day, returning to this house each of night at ten p.m. After this allotted time, I will never return.

When I arrive, for seven nights, I will walk down The Hall of Art and Pleasure to the left of this desk and select a door. I will stay within the room until the lights turn off.

On the eighth night, I will walk down The Hall of Temptation to the right of this desk to be tested. This will complete my education.

I understand that I will not be filmed or recorded in any way. All acts that take place in Maple House are completely confidential. I also understand that at any point, I may say, "Stop," and any experience I am a part of will immediately cease.

This contract is an offer based upon a need identified by one of our members.

There was a spot for my signature and the date. Underneath, the dates I was expected to be here were laid out, and it started ... tonight.

It didn't give a girl a whole lot of time to digest the information. This was ... what? A sex club? A stripper house? What kind of education? The words *sexual awakening* popped out at me. I needed to learn how to have sex? Was that what this was? I wasn't a virgin.

Except maybe I really was terrible at sex.

Sure, the stripper had been the one to give me the card, and maybe he was the member who had "identified" me, but what if ... what if it was actually Brayan?

I bowed my head in shame.

I was only twenty. Why did I have to be so great at sex? It wasn't like I'd been doing it for a long time. What was the big idea?

The contract loomed in front of me, a taboo promise, laden with mystery.

I understand I may leave at any time.

I unstrapped my pepper spray from my wrist and shoved it in my pocket, grabbing the pen. This wasn't like me. I didn't do stuff like this.

But it was college. If not now, when?

I signed my name at the bottom of the page. Then I froze, waiting for … I didn't know what I was expecting.

No one popped up and escorted me down the hallway. Nothing happened at all.

I got to my feet, turning toward the hallway to the left—The Hall of Art and Pleasure. And I was supposed to pick a door? How?

As I stepped into the dimly lit hall, it became clear that each door had a piece of paper attached to it. Okay then.

My analytical mind assessed the number of doors as I walked down the hall, planning on working from back to front before making my decision. If I hated all of them … then I'd walk out.

I deliberately ignored the papers until I reached the end of the hall. There were ten doors total, five on each side. I'd be picking seven. So, if I stayed, I could omit three of them.

I cautiously touched the piece of paper of the door nearest me, squinting at a rough hand-drawn picture of a woman suspended in the air by her arms, a man with a whip standing back with a sadistic smile on his face.

I dropped the piece of paper. Oh, hell no. No fucking way was I doing that. It was almost enough to make me want to walk out right then.

But I peered at a few more papers, and I saw the pattern. I'd walked all the way down the hall. Now that I turned around, the scenarios became less scary as I walked back toward the front door. Some papers had fragments of poetry, and others were paintings, hinting at what could be behind the doors.

In the end, I had a hard time choosing between two doors. One was probably about oral, if I had to guess. The painting was nothing more than a pair of lips. I hesitated for a second, but giving a blow job was low on my list of priorities tonight. I wasn't in the mood.

The other door ... I fingered the weathered paper again as I read the fragment of poetry.

> *Thy self: cast all, yea, this white linen; hence,*
> *There is no penance due to innocence:*
> *To teach thee, I am naked first; why then*
> *What needst thou have more covering than a man?*
>
> *—John Donne*

I hadn't exactly studied poetry, but *I am naked first* didn't really need to be translated. If I opened the door, would a nude man be standing there? Would it be the stripper from the night before?

I remembered the way he'd looked at me, all sexy and serious at the same time. I'd felt an instant connection with him, or I never would have let him handcuff me.

A full minute passed as I braced my hand against the handle, the desperate beat of my heart threatening to break through my rib cage. Then I twisted the knob and, in a rush, pushed through and slammed the door.

I stood, facing it a while before I dared to turn around. Would someone approach me?

No one did. *I can do this.*

I slowly turned, and the sight of the room stole my breath. I pressed my hand to my chest as I was transported to another time and place. Candles created a softly lit atmosphere. The room was draped in white silks that floated lazily in the breeze of a few fans. There was a canopied four-poster bed directly in front of me, and it was like … like *Arabian Nights*. Like I was Scheherazade or something. The walls were completely made of mirrors, making the room look larger and more elaborate, the bedroom reflected golden and beautiful on every wall.

This was the romance missing in my life. Not the hasty hookups that were so common in college. Not the way I'd lost my virginity in the back of a cramped sports car, all awkwardness and pain. This was a romance novel, a dream.

A low chuckle rumbled from the side of the room.

I turned, startled to see a man leaning back in an opulent chair, staring at me. His dark brown hair was pulled back. He wore a button-down white shirt and black slacks, like he had just gotten in from the office. Not naked after all. He appeared to be about twenty-five with kind hazel eyes and … wow. His legs were long. I'd never slept with someone who promised to be so tall.

I bit my lip. He wasn't the stripper from Cherries.

He gestured to the room with one hand. "You like it?" he asked in a mild tenor.

I nodded.

He unbuttoned the cuffs of his dress shirt, eyes downcast.

I twisted my hands together in front of my coat. This was so awkward! "So, the contract …"

He chuckled again but didn't say anything.

"Kind of crazy, huh? What exactly am I doing here?"

Having undone his cuffs, he moved on to his shirt with slow deliberation, but he didn't answer me.

"And how do you get to be part of a, um … this?" I asked, retreating until my back was flat against the door.

He pulled his shirt over his head and tossed it in a ball to the side of the room, then unbuckled his belt. It whipped through the loops of his pants, and he held it for a moment, his mouth quirked into a teasing smile before it hit the ground with a dull thud.

His eyes zeroed in on where my hand rested, just inches from the door handle. "Do you feel safe?"

I shook my head once. This man was anything but safe. This house? Completely unsafe. It was like some weird fever dream, the whole thing.

I could leave right now. If I wanted to.

I felt behind me until my fingers touched the doorknob.

The man paused in undressing, one hand on his zipper, his tanned skin glowing in the low light of the room. He arched an eyebrow.

It was almost like he could see the thoughts as they raced through my head.

Why did I sign that paper? I chose this room, but … I'm not ready. Am I? I squeezed my eyes shut.

"Mackenzie," he said softly, "we don't have to do anything you don't want to do, but there was a reason you said yes. A reason you chose my door. I get it if I'm not your type."

I opened my eyes. It was my turn to frown at him. He couldn't possibly doubt his attractiveness. His chest was toned, tapering into a flat stomach. He was the type of man who evoked the cavewoman in girls, the need to feel protected. A knot formed in my throat as I observed the trail of light-brown hair that began below his navel and disappeared into the band of his black trousers.

I shook my head, and his face fell.

"No, I didn't mean—" My hand left the knob, and I took a step forward.

His teasing smile was back, and I realized what he'd just done. He was messing with me, trying to get me to abandon my desire to flee to comfort him.

I folded my arms, slightly annoyed, but mostly amused. "Well played."

He bowed like an actor in a Shakespearean play with the flourish of an imaginary hat, managing to drop his pants at the same time.

I giggled. I couldn't help it. It was so smooth yet so funny.

When he straightened, the warmth in his eyes had changed. Now, they smoldered with something different, something primal.

Oh boy. What did I get myself into?

6

MIRRORS

The man was hilarious and hot, and I wanted to climb his body like a jungle gym. But … Brayan's face flashed in front of me. What if he found out?

I shouldn't care. Brayan had dumped me the second he got into my pants. Fuck him.

The man's thumbs played with the waistband of his black boxer briefs as he sauntered toward me. When he was less than five feet from where I still stood in my puffy coat, he halted. In a split second, he yanked down his underwear.

Holy crap. I wanted to shield my eyes, but that wasn't why I was here. *Be brave.*

He kicked the underwear away and continued to stalk forward.

I retreated until my back bumped into the door again.

Still, he advanced until my face was only inches from his very solid, very warm-looking chest.

My breath hitched as he lifted my chin with his finger.

"*I am naked first; why then, / What needst thou have more covering than a man?*" he recited flawlessly, backing away from me, his arms outstretched in an obvious challenge.

If this were a soap opera, the commercial would begin now. I'd be on the edge of my seat, waiting for the damn ads to end to find out if the two characters would have sex.

Maybe it was because I was angry with myself for trusting Brayan, and maybe it was because of the way this incredibly sexy man was looking at me, but I didn't want to leave anymore. Not even a little.

With shaking hands, I removed my hairband, letting my curls fall to my shoulders, untamed. I stared him down across the small space.

Challenge accepted.

And it was then that he truly smiled, white teeth bared to me.

"Are … are you going to help me undress?" Damn it, I didn't mean to sound so timid.

He shook his head, reaching an arm toward me.

I stumbled forward and took his hand, still managing to avoid looking at his, erm … well …

The tall, confident, very naked man led me to one of the mirrored walls to stand before our reflection.

My body was dwarfed in my extra-huge, puffy coat, my posture stiff and my skin as pale as ever in the dead of winter. But he was …

I couldn't help the fact that my eyes zeroed right in on his dick.

He was definitely turned on. I opened my mouth, ready to apologize for looking, but then snapped it shut. He was the one who stripped. It wasn't like I had walked in on him in the guys' locker room or something.

He bent down, lifting a curl off my shoulder. Our eyes met in the mirror.

"Am I ..." I licked my lips. "What are you supposed to teach me?"

"Undress," he whispered in my ear, staring me down through the glass.

Obediently, I unbuttoned my coat and let it fall to the floor. Then I kicked off my boots.

It wasn't exactly sexy, trying to get my hoodie over my head, and I struggled to stay in the moment, not to laugh as I balled it up and tossed it aside. At the same time, I was hyperaware of the fact that I wore no shirt underneath it. Only a bra.

He tugged on my strap when I paused.

I sucked in a breath. This was why I'd signed the paper, right? Right.

His stare burned into me as I unclipped the band of my bra and dropped it on the pile of clothes on the floor, but I couldn't bear to watch his face in the mirror. Were my boobs too small? Too pointy? He worked in a sex house, for God's sake. There was no way they measured up to all the boobs he probably saw on a daily basis.

His hot mouth came down to nibble on my shoulder. "Now, your pants."

I peeled off my skinny jeans and underwear at the same time, trying hard to make it look somewhat sexy when it most likely wasn't. Why on earth would I wear skinny jeans? They were the worst to try to strip out of. And was it horrible that I hoped, while bending over, my ass might brush against his legs?

His hand skated over my spine and down to the roundness of my backside as I yanked the fabric away from my ankles and stood.

His hand stayed where it was on my right butt cheek. He gave it a faint slap.

Despite the crazy situation, I giggled. I glanced behind him at the bed.

"Soon," he promised.

Then his entire body pressed against my back, hard and hot. His arms bracketed me in front of the mirror, my head cradled in the strength of his chest.

"Watch us," he rasped. And then his hands drifted down to my breasts, rolling my nipples between his thumbs and forefingers.

I arched against him, squeezing my eyes shut. He didn't start small, did he?

"You are so goddamn beautiful," he said. "Open your eyes, Mackenzie. Look."

I did. He was so tall, so gorgeous as his hands worked against my breasts.

"No. Look at you." His mouth stretched into a small smile.

My eyes shifted to my reflection. It was easy to see the imperfections I'd lived with for so long, the things I wanted to change about myself. My frizzy hair, the freckles on my skin, the roundness of my hips, the cellulite in my thighs.

But in this light, in this moment, I saw someone different. I saw a woman, naked and nervous, but brave as hell. My face flushed with excitement as he continued to touch me.

I'd never watched myself like this before, solo or with a partner. Goosebumps erupted over my body, and my nipples tightened. The sight of one of his hands dropping to my waist to skim lightly along my hip had my heart rate ratcheting up in anticipation.

The right side of my hip was sensitive, and when his featherlight touch reached the area, I couldn't keep myself from bucking slightly against him.

"A sweet spot, huh?" he whispered. "Let me help. Just watch." His other hand dropped to the same spot, both hands working against me until my knees went weak and my breathing morphed into uneven gasps.

His hand moved farther south. The skin he touched tingled in the wake of his hand as his fingers found my folds. He dipped in to stroke my clit.

"Ah!" I gasped as his finger lightly circled, bolts of arousal streaking through my body.

"Keep your eyes open," he ordered as his hand continued moving. "That's it." His other arm slipped under my knee and hiked up my leg, opening me up further.

My breath came in frustrated pants as I became slick against his touch. There was a heat building in me, and I needed …

"Please," I whispered. "Can we …"

"Place your hands on the mirror," he commanded.

I did as he told me.

His eyes locked with mine in the reflection. "Wait."

I nodded wordlessly.

His fingers left me as he lowered my leg. He retreated back to the center of the room.

My stomach clenched as I stared at myself in the mirror. Where was he? Above the soft whir of fans, the faint rip of a package sounded.

Oh. Condom.

He returned to my sight again, standing behind me. He smirked at my stance. I hadn't moved an inch, my hands now sweaty against the glass.

He again sought my eyes in the mirror. "Okay?"

I nodded once, knowing what I was agreeing to. When I swallowed, he watched the motion, his eyes glued to my throat. Then he yanked my leg into the air again, and his cock nudged my entrance.

Oh my God, we were actually going to do this.

He nipped my neck, and a chill raced through me.

Inch by pleasurable inch, he slid into me.

"Mmm," I hummed in a voice that sounded nothing like me.

"Still okay?" he asked in a tight voice.

"Yes," I gasped, my hands slipping a little on the mirror. My eyes were fixed on his expression, somewhere between the pain of holding back and the bliss of entering my body.

Slowly—oh-so achingly slowly—he withdrew and plunged back into me. I cried out. It was a good thing that my hands were braced against the mirror because each time he withdrew, his reentry caused me to see stars in the best possible way.

"Watch me, Mackenzie. Watch me fuck you. Own this moment."

My hands slipped against the mirror as I continued to do as he asked. I'd never felt ugly per se, but the word *average* came to mind.

Now, I watched as my breasts bounced when he thrust into me. My curls swayed in time with his movements. My mouth fell open as I panted, unable to keep my cool as the friction of our lovemaking aroused inside me a climb that I'd only ever experienced solo up until this point.

The sheets drifted behind us in an invisible breeze and framed our bodies in the mirror. The room smelled of fabric softener and vanilla. It was like something out of a smutty romance novel, and with this tall, sexy man behind me, I looked a lot like a woman on the cover of one of those books. It was empowering to see this woman—me—in the mirror.

I jutted out my ass, wanting to see myself be fucked. He turned me on, but I was turning me on, too.

I braced myself with one arm against the mirror, and as he pumped into me, I let the fingers of my free hand wander down to my clit.

His face was lined with concentration and pleasure. He watched me rub myself, even as he continued his hard rhythm.

A moan escaped my lips. My body tingled. I couldn't … I wanted …

"Yes, baby. Watch yourself take it," he said.

His words were enough to make me convulse. My hand fell to my side, and my knees buckled as ripple after ripple of my orgasm shook me to my core.

When my legs turned to jelly, he slipped out of me and scooped me up, throwing me onto the bed.

I laughed as my body bounced once, but it was a gasping sort of sound. It was almost too intimate, what we'd just done. Sex was different when I didn't come, but this man … he'd seen me lose all control.

My face heated, and I searched the bed for a blanket to shield myself.

He leaned against the bedpost, frowning down at me. "Anyone who fucks you should never want that gorgeous body covered."

I froze. Well, he certainly was comfortable naked. Was what he had said a line, a thing he was supposed to say that went with the poem? I didn't care.

He lowered himself to the bed and began to crawl toward me, stalking me through the silk sheets like he wasn't done with me yet.

Of course he's not done. He hasn't come yet. Which was new. All of this was new.

I didn't think to move until he was already upon me. He growled and grabbed me by my arms, pinning me down beneath him for a moment, and then in a skillful and surprising move, he flipped me on top of him.

And though I'd already orgasmed, I was turned on. Oh God, was I. And I wanted to see his face now when he lost himself inside me. I braced my hands on his chest as I rocked forward and enveloped him in one wet, fluid motion.

His eyes flew open. "Fuck," he said.

I stilled. *Did I hurt him?*

"No. Fuck," he groaned, reaching for my hips. "Don't stop."

I hadn't done something wrong. I'd done something hot. I licked my lips, rocking forward again, grinding against him. The pressure against my already-throbbing clit was overwhelming. I needed more. Soon, I forgot about giving him the ride of his life as I became more concerned with grinding hard enough to get the friction I needed to get myself off again.

I glanced over my shoulder at the mirror on the wall. Though I couldn't see myself in as great of detail as I had when he was fucking me against it, the image of me straddling this man, of me taking control, thrilled me. I could be confident. I could be sexy. Why shouldn't I? This was what it was all about, right? Even the swell of my hips seemed erotic right now.

"Yes, baby, use me," he said, his hands squeezing my thighs. "Holy shit, you are so good."

I almost fell off of him in shock. Was I?

He groaned again.

I bent forward to kiss him, thanking him the only way I could right now. *You are so good.* The exact thing I needed to hear after Brayan.

He grabbed my hips, thrusting up violently. He held me there, fucking me from below as our mouths mimicked the action.

He sped up, the friction sending me into absolute bliss.

Yes, more. God, more.

He was going to come, but I was getting there, too.

"I can't wait anymore," he ground out, his hips clashing hard against mine as he shuddered.

His dick swelled inside me, spasming, and it was enough to do me in again. He rocked into me once more, hitting that perfect place inside me as he continued to come.

I gasped, digging my nails into his shoulders. Then he reached forward, and the rough pad of his thumb grazed my clit. I came, harder this time. My yell was muffled against his chest, the salt of his sweaty skin against my tongue as I clutched him to me, needing an anchor. My hair encased my face in a thick curtain as my body shook.

Holy fuck.

I collapsed next to him.

We lay there together, just breathing, his arm curled protectively around me until goosebumps peppered my arms from the fans continuing their feathered breeze.

"Confidence," he finally murmured.

Then the lights flicked off, and he rolled away. For a moment, my hands hunted for him. There were so many things I wanted to say, to ask. Would I see him again? I couldn't let that kind of intense sex go, could I? But less than thirty seconds later, the lights flicked on, and he was nowhere to be found. I was the only one left in the room.

It was time for me to go.

It seemed terribly normal to refasten my bra and shimmy back into my pants, but that was my next step. I was all thumbs, and it took me longer than it should have to get dressed.

The empty room seemed brighter now, colder.

Once I was decent, I exited the room into the quiet mahogany hall and walked in a daze all the way back to my dorm.

The chill of the night air didn't touch me. I wasn't tired. All I could think was, *It was a sex house. A sex house!* That couldn't be legal. Well … it wasn't like I was prostituting myself or that they were … right? I had no way of knowing whether or not they were getting paid. But what I didn't know wouldn't kill me, right?

What in the actual fuck? What the hell was I doing?

I hadn't even dated anyone until I got to college, and now …

Stop it. That didn't matter.

But I knew it did. A lot of this sex stuff, this relationship shit, it was something people figured out in high school. But I hadn't.

I'd like to blame it on my upbringing, on the way my parents had made my curfew so early, being an only child, something. But I hadn't wanted any of the guys I went to high school with. I didn't see them that way. No one had seen *me* that way either. Not in my small town.

I flopped into bed after shucking my coat and boots when I got to the dorm, every bone in my body feeling like overcooked noodles. I didn't even check to see if Bliss was in the bed across the room.

Maybe I was overthinking this. What had Tristen said? I was intense. Maybe the house on Maple would make me loosen up. I could learn something from these encounters, though I didn't know what.

"Confidence," the nameless man had said.

Did I feel more confident?

A little thrill ran through me when I remembered the rough tenor of his voice when he'd muttered that final word. The image of him fucking me in the mirror. The absolute power of being on top of him, watching him fall over the edge into his own pleasure.

Every second of that had been undeniably hot, and I *did* feel more confident.

Holy shit, was I going to have sex seven more times this week with different people? Or the same person? That was a lot. How could I process something like that?

7

POLAR PLUNGE

It was easy to distract myself from thinking about The Hall of Art and Pleasure the next day.

Okay, fine. No, it wasn't. But I sure as hell was going to try.

My side of the dorm room overflowed with dirty clothes and a few dishes with half-eaten food in them. Empty ramen packages that had been thrown in the general vicinity of the trash earlier in the week were now crumpled in the corner, and the dead petals of the flowers Bliss and I had gotten from a greenery exhibition floated in the grungy water of the unwashed vase on the windowsill.

I was halfway surprised she hadn't killed me yet since pretty much all of it was my mess. I glanced at her perfectly made bed and sighed.

Time to clean.

I pitched the flowers, swept up, and even ran some Clorox wipes over the surfaces of the bathroom as a kind of sorry for her having to live with a slob. I took out the trash, washed the dishes, and spent some time studying in the common room as I turned over a couple of loads of laundry I didn't bother to separate into colors and darks.

When I got back to our room, Bliss was still gone, so I texted her.

> Me: Are you alive?

I cleaned for her. She should see it.

> Bliss: I should be asking you where you went last night!
> You slept forever this morning.

> Me: Are you coming home soon?

I picked up a bottle of air freshener and spritzed it in the general direction of the futon.

> Bliss: In a bit. I have a surprise for you!

Knowing Bliss, that could mean anything from she had gotten her nails done to she was joining the Peace Corps.

Ugh, I hated waiting. Waiting meant time to think, and I couldn't bring myself to think about what had happened last night, how I'd come more than once for a total stranger. How I might never see him again. Where did that leave me? And what about tonight?

I needed a distraction.

I could open my phone and spend time swiping right on guys I'd never have the guts to meet in real life. I could clean—*gulp*—the shower. Or …

I found myself walking down the hall to the events board. People tacked whatever they wanted to its surface—some trying to drum up members for their clubs, others announcing onetime events.

I skimmed the papers, pulling down a few that were a while ago and throwing them in a nearby garbage can. Then I saw it.

The Polar Plunge.

Jumping into freezing cold water with a bunch of other idiots on campus had never appealed to me before. They had to break the ice over the silly little pond near the university's entrance to even do the darn thing. There was also a dress code. You couldn't take the plunge in winter clothes or even a wetsuit. If you were a guy, you had to go in your swim shorts. And if you weren't a guy … I eyed the flyer. The few girls in the picture looked awfully blue, but also proud of themselves as they stood on the ice in nothing but flip-flops and bikinis.

You know what? Yeah. Hell yeah. Why not?

I marched back to my dorm and ripped open my dresser, scrounging through my top drawer until I found my electric-blue bikini. It never saw the light of day. I only owned it for occasional spray-tan purposes.

I dressed quickly, then threw my sweats back on while I waited for Bliss to get back from wherever the hell she was.

The moment she walked through the door, I hit her with it.

"I'm doing the Polar Plunge."

She burst out in laughter, shoving a copy of the same flyer I'd seen earlier into my hands.

"Huh?"

"That was the surprise, you dork." She chortled. "I was gonna enter! But now, we can do it together! Maybe we can get the rest of the floor to come and cheer for us."

"Um, sure."

Of course this kind of thing drew a crowd. My gut twisted.

"I can't believe you're willing to go. You never do things last minute."

I trailed behind her as she entered the bathroom, pulling her blonde hair back into a sleek ponytail. She wasn't wrong.

It was just that being brave had been good for me lately. Jumping into The Hall of Art and Pleasure wasn't something I regretted. It had been amazing. The look on that man's face as he'd watched me through the mirror was worth any discomfort I'd felt signing the contract.

"Is that—did you clean?"

"Hmm?"

Bliss sniffed the air. "It smells better in here. You tried to wash things! Thanks, Kenz."

She finished with her hair and hugged me hard.

I hugged her back absently.

"You okay? Cleaning and jumping into freezing water aren't really you."

"I'm fine, I swear. It was, like, two Clorox wipes."

"Alright then, bring on the pneumonia!" She sprinted into the hall and cupped her hands around her mouth. "Mackenzie and I are going to wear skimpy bikinis at the Polar Plunge in half an hour! Cheer us on or forever be on our shit list!"

I sighed. She had no filter. And I didn't even have a shit list.

Tristen's door cracked open, and he watched me drag Bliss back into our room. I gave him a dorky thumbs-up, and he threw his head back and laughed.

"It's so fucking cold. How did I let you talk me into this?" Bliss chattered a mere twenty minutes later.

We stood on the ice, wearing sweats, boots, and winter coats over our bathing suits with the other students willing to "take the plunge."

We'd actually paid twenty bucks apiece to do this craziness.

"All for charity," the skinny spokesman had said as he took our money, his pervy eyes trailing the length of our bodies, as if he could see underneath our coats.

I hugged mine close. "You came home with the idea!" I told Bliss. "You were already going to do it!"

Bliss snorted. "I wouldn't have gone through with it, though! You're supposed to be the voice of reason."

Maybe I didn't want to be the boring one all the time. Maybe I wanted to be someone else.

There were twenty-two of us idiots willing to jump into the pond. The crowd of spectators was huge, though. At least a couple hundred had shown up to watch.

I tried to ignore the stares as they chatted with each other in the cold, the noise of their voices a low background hum.

I almost looked for Brayan. But of course, he wouldn't be here. He didn't know I was doing this, and even if he did, we weren't dating anymore. He wouldn't believe I'd do something so brave.

Which was why I was going to do it.

The announcer spewed some crap about the tradition of our great university and the other dumbasses who had been stupid enough to do this in years past. Then some guys took pickaxes to the ice. As they broke it apart, I almost wished they had let the contestants do it. It looked like good exercise, and maybe it would have generated some heat.

To my left, a bulky guy, who apparently didn't need a coat or a shirt like everyone else, glanced at me. "So great we're doing this on a warm day!"

It was eighteen degrees out.

"Yeah," I said, trying to be polite. I turned to Bliss and raised my eyebrows.

She gave me a saucy look. "Trade with me, so I can flirt then."

"No. You're not bringing Crazy McMuscle back to our dorm," I hissed.

She giggled, her straight blonde hair blowing in the wind.

Everyone around us began pulling off their layers, so Bliss and I followed suit. We shed our coats, hoodies, pants, and finally shoes. The ice below my feet stung as I approached the dangerous-looking black water of the pond.

How deep was this anyway? What if I did it wrong? Would I be trapped under the ice forever?

My nipples compressed into marbled points, and I resisted the urge to cover my chest with both hands. *Just own it.* It was kind of hard to do, though. This was as naked as I had ever been outside, and it was in front of a mass of people. I hadn't thought this through at all.

McMuscle looked down at me, completely skipping my face.

"I love the Polar Plunge," he said mostly to himself.

I rolled my eyes, but I couldn't help but smile. A desperate laugh bubbled up within me.

"It's time for the countdown," the perky announcer crowed.

I could do this. I was going to do this.

Bliss gripped my hand, her perfectly manicured nails digging into my skin like cold little claws.

"Ow," I complained as a frigid breeze kicked up across the ice.

She let me go. "Sorry. I'm just excited."

My gaze skittered over the heads of the crowd and landed on a pair of cool gray eyes.

Tristen clapped together his mittened hands, shaking his head. *You're crazy*, he mouthed at me.

I shrugged, smiling big. At least I had one fan.

"Four ... three ... two ... one!"

I didn't think. I just jumped off the ice and into the pond.

The shock of the water was complete and intense. Air whooshed out of my lungs. And the burning! I knew that was my body thinking I was on fire when, really, I was just insanely cold, but, my God, it was horrific. My descent seemed to last forever, and my climb back to the top of the pond was an eternity, but as soon as I emerged, a hand reached down to help me.

Bliss, encased in her very warm-looking coat, not a hair on her head even the slightest bit damp.

I sputtered at her, unable to string together any words because of the cold.

Her expression was decidedly chastened as I struggled to climb out and roll onto the ice. As soon as I was upright, she wrapped me in both our towels.

"I chickened out, okay?" she said. "But you did it! You're such a badass!"

I tried to smile, but my lips weren't working right, so I nodded.

The muscly guy from earlier clapped me on the back. "You did it, crazy girl!" He shook his hair like a dog, spraying me with little bits of ice.

I laughed through chattering teeth. I had. I had done it.

The crowd opened up and swallowed us. All at once, we were surrounded by a bunch of people from our hall, each patting me on the back and calling me insane and laughing. I couldn't help but get caught up in the excitement. Bliss shoved me back into my sweats and coat, and before I knew it, I was riding the best adrenaline high as I pranced the short walk back to the dorm with the crowd.

"Your lips are blue," Tristen said as he fell into step beside us. "Are you okay?"

I'd worry about getting a cold later. I wrapped my hair back in my towel as we walked, then pulled my hood over the top of it. Chills rippled over my body, even as encased as it now was.

"Why? You going to warm her up?" Bliss drawled.

I pushed her off the sidewalk and into a foot of snow.

"Hey," she said. "These are new Sperrys!"

"They're boots," I said. "Use as prescribed."

Tristen and Bliss traded concerned looks over my head. Maybe I had chattered the last part, but it was okay. Because I was "crazy." Because I was a "badass." Because I was proud of myself, and I didn't want it to end.

"Want anything from Joe's?" Bliss offered, already digging in her pocket for money.

"Nah. Have fun, you big chicken." I just wanted a shower. A really hot one. No detours.

She stuck her tongue out. "Okay, see you guys later," she said as she split off from us. Apparently, the mere thought of having to jump in the icy water had her craving the scalding drink that passed for coffee at Joe's.

Which left Tristen and me walking back to the dorm together.

"So …" he said. "How's your studying coming?"

Crap. I still needed to study for that damn test. "Good. You?"

"Fine. You do this kind of stuff often?" He waved toward the pond.

"Jumping into stupidly cold water? Not so much." I shoved my mittened hands into my pockets for the extra warmth.

61

We hurried across a crosswalk at a four-way stop.

"So, why today?" he asked when we got to the other side of the street.

It was a good question. It would be easy to say I was bored, but that wasn't quite it.

"I've been a little stuck lately."

"Stuck how?"

Was this too deep to get into with a guy who was basically a stranger?

I increased my speed. "I don't know. You ever feel like the world is full of *shoulds*?"

He jogged to catch up to my pace. "So, you're a rule follower."

"Normally? Kinda, yeah. I just wanted to do something different." Because having sex with a random guy in a weird house was apparently not enough.

"The Polar Plunge is different—that's for sure."

I pressed the button at a stoplight. Pausing in the cold was so much worse when my hair was wet. "What about you? Are you a rule follower?"

He snorted. "Not exactly."

"Oh, that's right, Mr. I Don't Go to Class. What other rules do you break?" I teased.

"I can't stand peas," he said seriously.

The light turned to Walk.

"What?"

We picked our way carefully across the slick street.

"Hate 'em. They squish between my teeth. It's like eating little balls of sour mush."

"I don't think hating peas makes you a rebel."

"I wear socks to bed, too."

I gasped in fake outrage. "You do not."

"Do too. I even have fuzzy ones with foxes on them."

"So, you're not just a rebel. You're also a psycho."

He raised his eyebrows. "And you're probably the girl who puts her little popsicle toes on her boyfriend's legs."

"Are you asking if I have a boyfriend, Tristen from down the hall? You know I just broke up with someone."

Were we flirting? This felt like flirting.

"Hey, you never know. Rule followers are a hot commodity right now."

Now, it was my turn to snort. "Well, you can calm right down. I'm still single."

"You sound upset about it. Didn't we cover the *his loss* part of this conversation the last time we walked together?"

I nudged his shoulder with mine. "We were talking about you."

"Nice subject change. Really smooth." This guy didn't miss a beat.

"Are *you* seeing anyone?" I asked.

"See, now, that was direct. I am not."

I hugged myself as the dorm came into view. "You don't seem to care."

He held the door to our building open for me. "Maybe you're just bad at reading people."

"That is ... completely possible. Thanks for that." Now, my teeth were chattering so hard that I had to grit them to get them to stop.

We walked in silence to the elevator, but my shaking didn't slow much. I needed a really, really hot shower. And all the blankets.

No one else joined us. We were alone as the doors to the elevator shut.

I patted my now mostly frozen turban under my hood. "You'd think they could spring for some music in here."

"Everyone would just complain about it," Tristen murmured.

I watched him in the mirrored wall of the elevator. He was handsome with his blond hair and blond eyebrows. Broad shoulders, easy smile. The kind of smile that made you warm, even when you had been stupid enough to jump into a pond in the middle of January. His eyes met mine, and my breath stuttered to a stop.

Did he catch me checking him out?

He pressed his lips together, obviously trying to keep from laughing.

Oh God, kill me now.

The elevator dinged, and the doors slid open.

We exited. I opened my mouth to say something but closed it again.

"This was fun," he said as we reached his door. "See you around, Kenzie."

As soon as he disappeared into his dorm room, the cold of the pond overwhelmed me again. It seemed his smile held only so much magic.

That night, after a scalding shower and an internal pep talk that took all of ten seconds, I found myself back in front of the sex house … er, Maple House.

I marched right up to it, thinking to myself that it wasn't weird to enter if I looked like I belonged. And I was brave. Well, today, I was. I'd jumped into freezing water in front of, like, a million people. What could this house dish out that I couldn't take?

I watched a couple shuffle by, holding the leash of a fluffy little dog who needed a haircut, and I had a startling thought.

Do the neighbors know what goes on here? They couldn't ... could they?

Stop thinking about it, I told myself as I marched through the door. *Stop thinking about anything. For once in your life, be brave.*

This time, in the hallway, I didn't walk all the way down the hall. I knew I wasn't ready for the last scenes depicted.

I wasn't drawn to a door with a poem tacked to it tonight, but rather a crude black-and-white drawing of two boxers with gloves on, standing opposite each other. One was male, one female. The girl's hair was curly like mine, and maybe that was the reason I stood there so long. But maybe ... maybe it was also because the two boxers in the drawing were naked from the chest up. And maybe it was because the promise of physical exercise was something I needed today.

To work off the cold, I told myself.

But also because my body hummed with the excitement of being so reckless today. What other trouble could I get into?

It was interesting for sure. Aside from their lack of dress, the drawing didn't seem very sexy.

What does this have to do with anything sensual?

My mind wandered involuntarily to a personal training session I'd had my freshman year of college. My trainer's name was Caleb, and I remembered thinking, even as he'd taught me how to do the exercises, that the way our bodies moved seemed a little sexual. When I was squatting, I'd imagined his hands on my glutes, checking my form. I shook my head. Of course that hadn't happened. Not even close.

I shrugged and turned the knob. I wouldn't mind exploring that particular fantasy.

The room couldn't have been more different than my first encounter in The Hall of Art and Pleasure. A square boxing platform dominated the center of the room, those flexible bands stretched around the border. There was a set of black boxing gloves on a plain wooden table and a small gym duffel bag to the left of it. Atop the bag was another one of those strange business cards with gold writing, this time with only one large word typed across it.

Change.

I unzipped the bag and found only two very small garments inside. One was a sports bra, which was pretty close to my actual size, and the other a pair of thin, stretchy booty shorts.

Great. I stood there a moment, holding the scraps of fabric. What would they even look like on me? I was still losing the freshman fifteen.

Don't think.

I stripped quickly, my eyes scanning the room for someone who might be watching, but the room was quiet. Empty.

Pausing over the booty shorts, I wondered if I should still wear my underwear. Ultimately, I decided against it because they might peek through and ruin the effect. Hadn't I just been in a bikini in front of most of campus anyway? I could handle this.

When I was dressed, I shoved my clothes into the duffel and zipped it back up, plunking it on the table. I fastened my hair back with the elastic from my wrist, then grabbed one of the boxing gloves and started strapping it on.

Maybe it was the adrenaline, but I was feeling pretty badass until I got to the second glove. It was kind of impossible to secure when I only had one other marshmallowy fist to help.

The door behind me swung open.

A man entered, a little taller and a lot bigger than me. His head was shaved close, and his dark brown eyes regarded my efforts with no little amount of amusement. He was shirtless, and, Jesus Christ, was he ripped. Muscles upon muscles but proportionate. Were those indents near his collarbone called traps? I eyed him hungrily. He could trap me.

"Um …" My eyes flicked to the floor as my face warmed. Why was I suddenly so shy?

He chuckled, crossing over to me in a low-slung pair of name-brand joggers. He was barefoot, too.

He strapped my other glove in an impersonal, efficient way and walked toward the ring. When he threw another amused glance over his delicious shoulder, I realized I was supposed to follow him.

I jogged forward and ducked under the rope he pulled up for me.

From the ground, he grabbed a pair of padded punching mitts and clapped them together.

"Show me what you got," he said.

We were really doing this? I'd never punched anyone or anything in my entire life. I was tallish, but this guy could wreck me in the ring if he wanted to. He really wanted me to hit him?

I stood there, blinking at him.

"Oh, honey, you're perfect," he said, which made no sense whatsoever.

He crossed behind me and lifted one of my arms, showing me what a jab looked like. My skin prickled as his chest touched my back. When he used his arms and hands to show me a few more basic punches, like uppercuts and crosses, the sinews of his arms moved so fluidly that it was like a dance.

His voice was low and methodical in my ear. I couldn't help the goosebumps that arose on my arms and bare midriff when his hot breath continued giving instructions.

"Put your arm here," he told me for the third time. "You need to protect your face. Always protect your face."

I leaned into him. "Uh-huh," I could hear myself whisper breathlessly.

"And make sure there's tension in your arm. Here," he said, his warm hand supporting my biceps as he pressed my body into the proper stance.

"Okay," I said, trying to remember what he was telling me.

But the hardness of his chest pressed against my back distracted me, as did the damp pressure of his breath in my hair. I'd always laughed at movies where something like this happened, where someone showed the heroine how to do something when, ultimately, it would end in kissing or sex. Maybe I hadn't been completely fair about that scenario. My brain was like mush right now.

He broke away from me in one swift movement, every bit the no-nonsense trainer. "Got it?" he asked.

I shook my head to dispel the drunkenness of how close we'd been. What was I supposed to be learning here again?

My confusion seemed to amuse him.

A fierce, competitive smile spread across his face. "Alright, Mackenzie. Come get me."

8

WRESTLE MANIA

I went hard.

When my fist hit the black pad on the man's hand, his face snapped to me in shock.

A warmth spread through my chest as his mouth quirked up into a half-smile.

"Again," he demanded.

I blew a stray curl out of my face and punched again. He absorbed the blow and continued running me through the paces. It wasn't exactly difficult to see that the more aggressive I was with my shots, the bigger the dark tent became in his pants. He was getting off on training me then? Or me hitting him? Either way, it was kinda hot.

Every time my fist flashed out, it was turning me on, too. The way his pupils dilated, the way he licked his lips once, twice.

"That's it, Mackenzie. Harder," he said. His eyes were on my breasts now as we circled each other.

"Is that how you like it?" I panted. A drop of sweat slid down the back of my neck.

He glanced down at his pants after deflecting another punch. "Hard is not a problem, honey."

I couldn't contain my smile.

"If you can land one on me, I might go easy on you," he taunted.

I paused a moment, and he used the opportunity to swipe at my face. I ducked.

"Nice dodge."

"I never said I wanted you to go easy."

He regarded me warily. "Then show me what you're made of."

So I did. Jab, cross, uppercut. We fell into a rhythm, but I wasn't playing. Sweat rolled off me, but I didn't care.

It was like I was hitting all the things that hadn't gone right this year. This hit was for the pitiful B-minus I'd gotten in Bio when I knew more answers than the professor.

The next strike was for all the times I'd blown off Bliss to hang out with Brayan when he never had any intention of seeing us through. She was my best friend. Why would I do that?

This one was for how naive I was.

That one was for trusting anyone ever.

Every blow I dealt, he deflected, and it was starting to make me mad. I wanted to land one, just one on him.

The game became more frustrating when he ditched the pads and used his bare hands. Every time I missed a hit, he found a way to land a soft touch on me. A slap to my mostly exposed ass. A light pinch to my side. A caress to the underside of my breast.

I lost my cool and went all out, trying to hit, kick, or punch anything of him I could reach.

"Finally," he said when I landed a hit on his shoulder.

He turned me around and held my arms to my sides, both of us panting.

"I want you," he said through gritted teeth. "Right here. Right now. But I don't want this to stop."

He didn't want what to stop? Us fighting? Fuck, that was hot.

"Then let me go," I panted back.

He released me.

I whirled around and jumped on top of him. He managed to cushion the blow for both of us as we fell to the floor, but I didn't care. I grabbed his hands and pushed them to the mat above his head. We both knew it was a useless gesture. His arms were almost as thick as my thighs.

"Got ya," I singsonged.

He growled and surged forward until my back smacked the padded floor.

Then unexpectedly, he wrenched me around so that my face was to the mat and my ass in the air, bracketed between his knees.

"I don't think so," he said in my ear as he put his whole weight on me. "You're pinned."

I tried to laugh, but it came out more like a wheeze. "I thought we were boxing."

"We're doing whatever I say we are," he countered, moving his weight suddenly from me.

There was a tug and a loud ripping noise. Cold air hit my backside. He'd just destroyed the seam of the thin boy shorts I was wearing.

"Are you going to—"

"You want me to?"

I nodded at the floor.

"I'm wearing protection," he muttered.

Half a second later, he was in me.

"Holy fuck, you're wet," he said.

My face heated. I tried to wiggle away.

"You're perfect," he breathed, pinning me back in place, pumping into me hard and fast.

It was almost embarrassing how close my orgasm already was, my face smashed against the floor, my body tired from fighting.

Still, I wasn't ready to submit, so I fought for the top position. He didn't relent, his calloused hands rough and unyielding as he forced me back down. The rhythm he kept all the while was bringing me closer to the edge.

My orgasm hit hard. I arched my back as a primal yowl escaped me. My knees shook with the force of it.

He stopped, breathing hard, giving me a second to adjust.

It was the opening I had been looking for. I pushed him onto his back. "Round two."

He smiled that way guys smiled when they got what they wanted. Then he tucked his hands behind his head, completely comfortable with his own body.

I wanted to smack that stupid smirk right off his face, but I hesitated. I'd always wanted to ride a man backward, and in that moment, I finally had the confidence to try. I sank back down on his impressive length, my body still wet and ready from our last tryst.

His breath hissed between his teeth.

I braced my knees on the floor on either side of him and started a quick pace. God, how had I never tried this position before? It pushed him in at an angle that perfectly hit that special place inside me.

"Holy shit," he said, and I heard a thump.

When I looked behind me, his head had fallen to the floor. I laughed, but it wasn't a girlie giggle. It was the sultry laugh of a woman.

"Touch my ass," I said.

He did, his fingers quick to dig into the flesh of my glutes as I slammed down on him again, again, again.

"Yes, oh God, fuck, I'm going to come."

"Do it," I growled as I rocked forward, the friction of his balls against my clit reigniting my own arousal.

His body bucked under me, and he shuddered. For a few moments after, I lay on top of him, just trying to breathe.

Holy shit, that was intense.

Finally, I shifted off of him and rolled away, but he wasn't … he was still hard.

"Ten percent," he said when I hopped up. "Ten percent of men can keep an erection." He stood and pulled the used condom off, chucking it to the side of the room. "Do you want to keep going?"

My body ached from the exercise and the hard floor. My calves and thighs burned from the way I'd ridden him with abandon. But as he fished another condom out of the sweatpants on the floor and rolled it over himself, he watched me with eyes that still shone with lust.

I couldn't help it. It was so damn sexy. My body was practically screaming, *Fuck yes. Let's do this.*

And he knew it.

Walking purposefully, he flexed his jaw as he stared down at the sheen of sweat on my body. He pulled off my ruined shorts in one violent motion. His hands ran up the backs of my legs and under the curve of my backside as he stood up.

"Jump," he growled.

So I did. He caught me as I wrapped my legs around him. Then he positioned himself at my entrance.

I bit his shoulder when he started fucking me again, lifting my ass up and down as he thrust into me so hard and deep that I saw stars.

His hands spread my cheeks apart, and his cock sank even deeper into me. I felt a small pressure before the tip of his finger pressed against my ass. I jerked against him, and the finger sank in deeper. The sensation was so foreign; the pressure, in combination with his hard cock spearing up into me, was almost too much to take. I held on tight to him as my legs shook, completely at his mercy.

"Arrghhh," he said. "You're so … I'm so …"

But I couldn't concentrate on what he was saying even if it had made sense. I was too far gone into a sexual mind space I couldn't identify.

He shifted, and then his fingers were on my clit, massaging, his rough hands bringing me right back to the edge.

Then I was coming again, a whimper escaping my lips.

He groaned low and guttural into my ear, then pushed into me so hard that it was all I could do to cling to him. His body shuddered with the strength of his own orgasm.

When his pleasure abated, he held me tightly for a second. Then he untangled my legs from his waist and set me on my feet. My legs were as wobbly as jelly as he led me back to the table where the duffel with my clothes lay.

I turned to him, searching his face for an answer to a question I couldn't even fully form. "I—"

The room went black, and his hand slipped out of mine. "Confidence," he said softly.

When the brightness returned to the room, he was gone, and I was exhausted.

My eyes were bleary as I settled into a seat in the last row of Economics the next day. As unnoticed as I was in that class now, I wanted even less attention, even more space between Brayan and me.

As the professor passed out the blank tests, Tristen slipped into the room and sat next to me. He grabbed a paper at the last second and winked.

"Study the captions?" he asked.

No. I had been too busy being fucked by some nameless guy in a house of sex.

I cleared my throat and began to read to the test in front of me. Tristen finished way before me and left. In fact, most of the people in the lecture hall finished before me. I took every last second to go over my answers, feeling a solid B in my future. That wasn't so bad.

I might have been tired and underprepared for this test, but I couldn't stop going to The Hall of Art and Pleasure. Something about it compelled me. I was already a little more confident with the men there. It was only a week and a day after all. It couldn't completely derail my studies in that time. And then …

And then what? I would have slept with eight men? Was that supposed to be an accomplishment? The card had said *For Educational Purposes Only*. What was I supposed to learn from fucking a bunch of guys?

I dropped the test off at the professor's desk. He was already grading, and he murmured a thanks as I trudged back up the stairs and exited the room.

Tristen was waiting on the bench across from the exit, and I could hear the *ping, ping, ping* of whatever game he was playing on his phone.

"You doing anything tonight for dinner?" he asked me without looking up. "Because I was thinking that you, me, Bliss, and my roommate, Tony, should go to the dining commons and create the world's largest nacho tower. Then we should Jenga the pieces down and eat them. Whoever collapses the tower has to buy everyone the first round tonight."

I laughed. How would that even work without breaking the chips? It sounded fun actually.

"I kinda have somewhere to be later. Like nine thirty," I said.

"Got a hot date?" he asked, squinting at the sun as we walked out of the dim building.

Light changes always made me sneeze. I struggled to hold it in, itching my nose. "Not exactly."

A long pause extended between us, but I wasn't willing to lie to him, and I definitely wasn't going to elaborate.

"So, nachos," I said, "should definitely happen. But I might not make it for the drinks. I don't know yet." I smiled up at him.

He grinned back, and the bottom of my stomach dropped out of my body in the best way when he threw his arm around me.

"I knew you'd see the light at the end of the friendship tunnel," he joked.

We stayed that way for a moment as we walked, his arm around me, but it was hard for me to match his touch with the words coming out of his mouth. All this time, I'd thought I was being the mean one, telling him that I couldn't date. But when he used the word *friendship* like that … I winced. It shouldn't have bothered me.

I wasn't one of those girls who wanted guys to like me without wanting anything to do with them, was I?

No. I was just going through a thing. Tristen was hot, which wasn't his fault. My body was reacting, which wasn't my fault. I could blame hormones and the fact that I was so sexually amped up.

Bliss squealed when I got back to the dorm and told her we were to meet Tristen and his roommate in the dining commons. We both pretended that doing our hair and makeup to go eat was normal. When we got to dinner, we both looked natural in that way that only an hour of preparation could make us appear.

If Tristen noticed, he didn't say anything, but he did sit next to me as we constructed the nacho tower, his face lined with concentration as he balanced one chip after another, using the nasty cafeteria cheese as a gloopy glue.

And even though it was a childish thing to do, it was fun. His warmth seeped through his long-sleeved shirt into my arm as we brushed against each other in our quest for nacho glory.

Bliss was having fun, too. She blushed when Tristen's roommate, Tony, sat down next to her, and I could see why. As much as Tristen was my type in that clean-cut, chiseled-face type of way, Tony was Bliss's type—all muscle with a big, booming voice and a presence that dominated every conversation.

Tristen and I were content to work on the tower, but Bliss and Tony might as well have been in a different world. They talked about anything and everything, and half the time, they knocked over the tower when using their hands in an effort to explain every little thing about their lives. It took a pretty self-confident guy to match Bliss's headstrong personality. Tony might be kind of perfect.

I tried to ignore the bolt of jealousy that lanced through me at their instant connection. I could also feel Tristen's eyes on me. When I caught him in the act, he didn't look away. He matched my gaze, looking for something I didn't know how to give.

A minute later, I frowned. I shouldn't be sharing meaningful looks with someone I wasn't interested in, should I? I didn't want to lead him on. He was the one who had said *friendship*.

As soon as the tower reached eye-level, we began the task of nacho Jenga, deconstructing it piece by piece, eating the chips as we went.

In an underhanded move, I ate the last stable chip.

"Kenzie, you fiend!" Tristen cried in mock outrage when it was his turn. "There's nowhere to go with this!"

His fingers probed the soggy mess.

"Guess you'll just have to buy me a drink then, huh?" I smiled, proud of myself.

"I would have bought you a drink anyway," he muttered. Too soft, I thought, for him to have wanted me to hear.

I let it pass.

When the nachos toppled down, Tony's roar of anguish and my victory wiggle were enough to make Tristen and Bliss chuckle with us.

"Fine, I've got the drinks," Tristen said as he wiped the cheese off his fingers with a flimsy cafeteria napkin.

I bounced a little with happiness before I remembered I couldn't stay for that. This night was already so fun that I was seconds away from quitting the house altogether. Tristen would never know. Maybe we could …

Who wants to date a girl who's terrible at sex? a mean voice inside me asked.

Tristen didn't exactly look like the type who didn't know his way around a bedroom. Not with those looks and that confidence. I needed The Hall of Art and Pleasure. The house could fix me.

"Um …" I debated.

But I couldn't end this journey right now. The sex the past two nights had been … well … and the rooms would only get more intense. And Tristen … despite the friendship vibe he was trying to put off, I could tell that for him, it was more than that. And maybe it was for me, too. And that was a really, really bad idea when I didn't know what I wanted right now. I was recovering.

"I have to be somewhere, remember?" I said after an awkward moment.

"Mmhmm," Bliss said, and I could tell she wanted desperately to ask me, but she was restraining herself.

Tristen nodded. "Me, too, actually, but I should be back in time for some late-night fun."

"Oh," I said.

Everyone waited for me to agree, to say the same thing, but I didn't. Who knew how long The Hall of Art and Pleasure would take?

I shrugged, and they let it go.

I felt like total shit.

9

QUICKIE

I hesitated on the sidewalk in front of the house on Maple. Wind sliced through my coat, lifting my hair, and chilling my bare legs under my skirt. Tristen's disappointed face flashed in front of me.

You made your decision. Just do it.

I opened the door.

In The Hall of Art and Pleasure, my fingers brushed the paper of one of the doors. I could've gone backward, stepped into the room that was obviously about oral sex, but this one called to me. It didn't seem quite so safe. A dark energy thrummed through me. Maybe I needed to make this night worth it, worth the fact that I had ditched Tristen and the others.

From "The Platonic Blow": Unclaimed Poetry
(but everyone knows it was Auden)

We aligned mouths. We entwined. All act was clutch,
All fact contact, the attack and the interlock
Of tongues, the charms of arms. I shook at the touch
Of his fresh flesh, I rocked at the shock of his cock.

Whoever had written this, typed this, or whatever must have been a literature major, one with a sense of humor. The title was funny. If I had been a poet back in ye olden days, I wouldn't have claimed the poem either.

Did the *shock of his cock* mean surprise sex? How could I be surprised if I knew I was going to get sex when I walked through the door?

I couldn't deny it was a fantasy of mine. One I had imagined sometimes when I had alone time to find my own release. What would it be like to be approached and immediately get down to business? To not know it was coming? No foreplay, just fucking. That would fit my mood perfectly today.

I shifted from foot to foot. Even if it wasn't technically surprise sex, I was ready.

I inched the door open, and darkness from inside the room spilled into the hall. How was I supposed to—

The doorknob was yanked from my hand, and I was pulled inside. The door slammed shut behind me. Pitch-black surrounded me. I was blind.

As I groped my way along the walls, it took only a few moments for me to realize this room was padded. It was also small. Ridiculously small. It was no larger than a closet!

My first instinct was to panic. I'd never thought I was claustrophobic until this moment, but the walls were so close. Too close. My heartbeat banged through my body, fast and unsteady.

"Shh," I heard. "Don't you think I'll take care of you?"

A man's arms encircled my body and squeezed. One by one, my tense muscles relaxed. When I was limp and my heart rate returned to normal, his bear hug loosened. I turned around in his arms.

His mouth settled on mine. The kiss wasn't rough by any means. It was beautiful, just the right amount of pressure. Open, but not demanding. Sweet almost.

"Can I have you?" he asked politely as his lips traced down my neck to my shoulder.

I nodded against him in the dark. Everything was heightened here. The goosebumps on my arms from his treatment of my neck, the way my body already tingled and throbbed at the thought of this stranger fucking me in what was basically a closet. I raised my hands to brush against his face, but he caught them with his and threaded his fingers through mine.

His knee parted my legs as he pushed me against the padded wall of the room.

"Mmm," he said. "You're wearing a skirt."

I smiled into the blackness of the room, knowing he couldn't see it. Did he even know what I looked like? Would I ever see him? I didn't care.

When his knee applied pressure at my most sensitive spot, I gasped.

His rough hands cupped my ass. "And a thong." He groaned.

I giggled. He acted like I'd just handed him the best present in the world for his birthday.

His mouth came down on mine again, tasting my smile. This time, he was less gentle, and I met him halfway.

He flipped me around and pressed me against the wall. He was really playing up the alpha thing right now, and not only did I not hate it, but my brain was also already imagining him fucking me to oblivion in half a dozen different positions. The sound of both of our rough breaths in the closed room was enough to make me so wet that it was embarrassing.

He flipped up my skirt and pushed my thong to the side. Then in one swift motion, he pressed into me.

Shock was an understatement.

My thong tugged against his dick as he slammed into me over and over, my own cries seeming to expand his cock and make him thrust harder.

"You're drenched," he said, his mouth nipping at my ear as he continued railing me. "You want me to fuck you and leave." It was such a dirty thing to say, but he wasn't wrong.

His hand slid around my hip and shoved its way under the front of my thong to touch my clit.

"Beg me to come," he growled, forcing my back to arch as he pulled my hair with his other hand.

"Please," I gasped. "Please … ahhh—"

His finger pressed harder as he circled my clit, increasing speed until I couldn't hold on anymore.

My orgasm overwhelmed me as I shuddered against him.

"God, yes," he said. "Squeeze me. Make me come, too."

He pounded into me, and we lost ourselves in the violence, in the darkness. Then he stuttered to a halt, resting his forehead in the cradle of my shoulder for a moment before pulling out.

His hand released my hair, and I panted against the padded wall. His arms nudged me back around until we were face-to-face, and I had that same overwhelming need to touch him to see what he looked like. I didn't, though. That wasn't what this room was about.

He pressed a quick kiss to my mouth. "Confidence."

I felt him leave rather than heard or saw it. I straightened my clothing, though I was already mostly put together. Quickie was right.

Thirty seconds later, the door unlatched, and the soft light from the hallway spilled in.

I shoved my frigid hands into my coat pockets the second I emerged from the house and quickened my pace against the unforgiving cold.

Confidence. Again? Really?

That was the lesson then. I couldn't ignore it a third time. But I never would've fucked someone I didn't know before this experience, let alone someone I'd never seen. It was almost as if the hall was giving me permission to let all kinds of sexually deviant things happen to me.

I chuckled. Sex in the dark was hardly deviant.

The house's challenge loomed before me. Night after night of sex, then some sort of test. I didn't know how to pass it or what it would even entail. How could I prove I was confident? How could someone even measure that?

I pushed the thought aside as I entered the warmth of the dorm. There was no use stressing about it when everything to do with the house was a surprise. I'd just have to deal with whatever it was when the night came.

I thought about trying to sneak back into my room, but it was only ten forty-five, and Bliss hadn't even left to go drinking yet. I hadn't considered that I could still go out. I hadn't lost the great nacho challenge. Tristen had, and now, he could pay up. It would be pretty chill, too. Not many people went out on a Monday night.

When I opened the door, Bliss looked up at me from where she was pregaming on the futon with Tony, passing a fifth of raspberry vodka back and forth. My stomach turned when I saw the label. If

I drank something like that, I'd be puking within an hour. Bliss's gut was made of steel.

"Where were you?" she slurred.

Great. I'd been gone for less than an hour, and she was already at the *too honest* stage of drunkenness.

"You keep leaving at night. It's been, like, a million times in a row."

I rolled my eyes.

She sat up, the clear liquid in the glass bottle sloshing forward. "Oh my God, are you dating a professor or something? Can you get me an A?"

I sighed but didn't answer her question. "Didn't take as long as I thought," I said, smoothing over my actual whereabouts.

Between my legs, my soaked thong was making me uncomfortable.

"Give me a second in the room to change, and I can be ready to go."

Tony grinned at me, and I couldn't resist smiling back. His happiness was contagious.

"Well, hurry the fuck up because we still have to go get Tristen," Bliss whined.

I eyed the way Tony's leg brushed against hers on the couch as they continued taking small swigs from the bottle. If I left them alone, would I need to shield my eyes when I came back out?

Bliss snapped her fingers in front of me.

"What? Oh yeah. Sorry," I said and shut the door that connected the common room to the bedroom.

I shed my clothes, including the wet thong, and put on sensible underwear and a different skirt—plaid instead of the black I'd worn earlier. I shook my hair out and threw a little hair spray on the roots, flipping it back up. It still looked pretty good from earlier despite the rushed sex at Maple House. Using the mirror that hung from the back of the bedroom door, I applied some bright red lip gloss that would wear off with one drink.

None of that distracted me from the whirling thoughts in my head, though. *What am I doing in The Hall of Art and Pleasure? Am I getting better at sex, so Brayan will like me? Or am I gaining confidence, so I can go out and get some other guy, like Tristen?*

Neither of those reasons felt true anymore. Somewhere along the way, it had become about me.

"Come *on*," Bliss yelled from the other room.

I took one last look in the mirror. I needed to stop overthinking things. College was supposed to be about fun. What was more fun than going drinking with two hot guys?

I reentered the main room. "Let's do this shit!"

Tony and Bliss cheered drunkenly.

"There's my Polar Plunge girl!" Bliss yelled as she jumped to her feet, then swayed and had to grab Tony's shoulder for support.

Oh man. I could already see the future of this night. We'd be bringing her back to this room to puke pretty soon.

I waited until Tony stood to see if he swayed the way Bliss had, but he seemed steady enough.

"Tristen!" Bliss yelled down the hall.

"Bliss, shh," I reprimanded her. "What if people are sleeping?"

When we got to the boys' door, Tristen was nowhere to be found. Tony texted him to meet us there, and I called an Uber.

This is good, I told myself. Tristen was too easy to talk to, too intense to ignore. He never even checked his phone when we walked together. It was like speaking with me was the most important thing he could be doing. That was dangerous.

Then why did my stomach sink at the thought of a night out, dancing with only Bliss and Tony?

We didn't go to the normal sports bar Bliss and I frequented. She said she wanted to dance because of course she did when she was this drunk. I tried to point out that there would be nowhere for us to do that this early in the week, but she had a plan. Even drunk, that girl always had a plan.

"There's a new club open tonight! They were super popular last week!"

Tony went along with it when I would have protested. Booths and beer were way more my scene. But Bliss was Bliss, and we did as she bid us.

Our fake IDs were accepted without a backward glance at the door of the dance club. Strobe lights and dry ice spilled out into the street as we entered, the bass from the speakers thrumming through the crowd. As soon as we walked through the door, we were hit with the overwhelming smell of AXE body spray and sweat.

"I almost wanted them to reject us," Tony confided to me. He was so tall that he had to bend down to talk to me.

Bliss glared at me when she saw it.

I smiled at her, trying to reassure her drunk brain that he was all hers. I was getting along well with his dry comments in the way that people got along when they were still sober and taking care of their tipsy friends.

"How long have you known Tristen?" he asked as we walked toward the bar.

Bliss was leaning over, yelling, "Sex on the Beach!" at an impressive volume.

It was making us look as underaged as we were, but whatever. We were already through. No one would turn us away now. It was too much effort.

"Like, a day or two." I laughed.

"Huh," Tony said, looking toward Bliss as she ordered us all shots.

"And he's paying!" she screeched at the poor bartender. "Because he lost the nachos!" She pointed to a guy at the bar.

Tristen.

He looked completely different in a solid blue button-down shirt and dark jeans. His hair was brushed neatly, like he'd just showered. Had he been at the gym or something? He couldn't have showered in the dorm. We had just been there.

"Are you and Tristen close?" I asked Tony. "I mean, you're roommates." We were far enough away from Tristen that I knew he wouldn't hear me even though I had to yell to be heard over the music.

"Yes," Tony replied simply. "Are you and Bliss close?"

"Yes," I said.

We looked at each other for a moment, perfect understanding flashing between us—*don't fuck with my friend*.

"Alright, lovers, cut that out," Bliss said, her voice sharp and completely inappropriate. "Do your shots because *Tristen* and I would like to dance."

I glanced at Tristen, who was being pulled along by the hand by a belligerent Bliss. He definitely did not look like he wanted to dance.

Tony and I tossed our shots at the same time, flipping the glasses face down on the bar and following them to the dance floor.

The beat was pretty sick, and the DJ had packed the place with college kids looking for a good time. Way more people were here than I'd thought would be, but I guessed a new club, combined with a college town, was a big draw. Hands wandered, high heels faltered, and the energy pumped through us. It was hard not to get caught up in the fun of it.

Warmth spread through my body from the shot. I wasn't exactly a lightweight, but it must have been a pretty high proof. Poor Tristen. That couldn't have been cheap.

I didn't go out with Bliss to dirty dance very often, but when we did manage it, those were some of my favorite nights. I threw my hands over my head and swayed my hips.

"Damn, Mackenzie! Shake it!" Bliss screeched from my left.

"Bliss—"

She was out of control.

"I got it. I'll get her home," Tony said.

I locked eyes with him again, a clear warning.

"I got it," he repeated, this time his meaning entirely different.

"You better," I muttered, hoping he could read my lips through the crowd.

His head came down in a curt nod, acknowledging my reluctance. We really didn't know these guys that well.

Then he led Bliss from the dance floor and back to the confines of a barstool while he requested an Uber.

Tristen and I were left to stand there awkwardly.

"Um," I said, but my body was still moving a little to the beat. I mean, I couldn't not.

"One more shot." He snagged a couple of tubes from a waitress walking by.

She looked him up and down, her eyes taking in his dress shirt and haphazard hair.

Oh, brother. I put my hand on one hip as I waited for him to talk to her.

She leaned into him as he said something in her ear, probably just giving her his name for the tab.

When he turned back to me, he chuckled.

I dropped my arm self-consciously.

He arched an eyebrow.

Smug bastard.

"Cheers," he said, handing me a tube.

We both drank the blue liquid, our eyes locked on each other. If this was a challenge, I didn't intend to lose.

But the drink was strong. Like, holy shit, was this straight gasoline?

"Oof," I joked.

"Ack," he replied.

And then, with liquid courage and the excuse that we were drinking, we danced. With my ass against his crotch, we found a dirty rhythm, which lasted well past the first song.

Tristen's hands stayed respectfully on my thighs and hips, not straying to more dangerous areas. But, damn, he was good.

It was hot in here, and I wanted to feel hot tonight, too. I placed one of his hands against my stomach and the other near my ass, and he laughed. Then he pulled me tight against him when the song told us to drop it low. As we sank closer to the floor together, pressed intimately against each other's bodies, my ass bumping against his obvious erection in the most sensual dance I'd ever had in a club, I couldn't help wondering how much of it was because he was drinking and how much was because he wanted me.

I laid my head back against his neck as his hands gripped my shirt and slid against my bare midriff. It was so sexual, the bulge of how much he wanted me pressing against me through his jeans.

I never wanted it to end, but after another song, I needed a break. Dripping in sweat, I whirled around to tell him, but the words got stuck in my throat. It was a lot easier to be naughty when we weren't facing each other.

He pushed a sweaty curl behind my ear. "Let's drink." He led me back over to the bar, where Bliss and Tony still stood.

"I thought you were going home," I shouted over the music.

"Big demand for rides," Tony grunted, nestling Bliss closer to him so she didn't have to stand on her own.

I drowned the shot Tristen ordered for me and leaned on him the way Bliss leaned on Tony. Tonight, I could almost forget that I couldn't have him. I was fucking other guys. I was learning to be "confident."

When the Uber finally came, the silence closed in.

All I could concentrate on the whole way home was the way Tristen's body pressed against mine in the small space of the backseat and the voice in my head that chanted, *User, user, user,* with every turn we took.

10

WRECK LESS

When my alarm blared at eight forty the next morning, I groaned and hit snooze a third time.

"Get up," I whispered to the ceiling. "Get up."

I swung my legs over the side of the bed, feeling boneless. Pulling my pants over my thighs was basically impossible, and I slammed my toe into the post of my bed as I tried to shimmy them on. With my jeans still around my legs, I collapsed onto my desk chair and swore.

Ten minutes later, I staggered out of my dorm room. My hair wasn't brushed, but half the time, brushing made my hair worse, so whatever.

Exhaustion pulled at my every move. I could've easily taken the day off, but Tristen was right about me. I was a try-hard. I sat in the middle in my Biology lecture and then noticed in lab that my table was in the center, too. God, was I that easy to peg? There was something to forcing myself to keep to a routine, though. By the time I left lab, I was fully awake and glad I wouldn't have to do makeup work for missing class.

As I slogged along the sidewalk back to my dorm to eat lunch, a light snow fell on the recently salted pavement. Winter was beautiful. So unpredictable, but always so pretty. My breath puffed out in front of me, and I clapped my mittened hands together. Students flowed around me as I passed by the English building. Most of them walked briskly, trying to get to another class or just to get out of the frigid air. Usually, that was me, but not today.

I stuck my tongue out to catch a fluffy flake and giggled when it took me a few tries to get one. I didn't remember this being as hard when I was a kid. Wouldn't it be fun to have a snowball fight? Who would even do that with me?

Tristen would.

I had to admit I was starting to like him. Last night was one of the most fun things I'd ever done. I could still feel him behind me, cradling me as we danced so dirty that my mom would have had a heart attack. The nervous, excited way my heart fluttered still lingered.

Back at the dorm, I hummed as I shook out my hat and hung up my coat.

Bliss was huddled in a blanket on the futon, clicking through the channels on our tiny TV. "How are you not hungover right now?" she groaned.

Aw, poor thing. "Do you need some Tylenol? I can get you some."

She shook the bottle at me from the couch.

I grabbed my Economics book from the shelf and sat next to her. "Whatcha watchin'?"

She turned off the TV and turned to me. "Why are you so happy? Oh my God, are you going out with Tristen?"

"Nope," I said cheerfully. "I don't even know the guy."

"Sure looked like you knew him last night." She wiggled her eyebrows.

My face heated. "Oh, please. How would *you* know, Miss I Drank Too Much Before the Club?"

"Because that boy was all over you. And I might have seen him in the hall ten minutes ago ..."

I groaned. Just like Bliss to get involved. "He said he wanted to be friends." Sort of. He'd dropped the *friendship* word, but he never completely shut down that avenue of thinking in either of us.

"Then he lied."

I rolled my eyes. "I'm allowed to be in a good mood without it being about a guy." I plugged my phone into the speaker dock and scrolled to an upbeat song.

She smiled because she knew what was coming. Whenever one of us had something to celebrate or was in a good mood, it was the other's responsibility to join in a dance party.

She stood up and stretched. "You have to do this when I'm hungover. Alright, bitch. Let's dance!"

We climbed on the none-too-sturdy futon and shook our butts to the dirtiest rap I could find, the music blaring down the hallway. Our moves started silly and got progressively more ridiculous, both of us laughing our asses off.

I jumped off the couch and slipped on the floor, falling into a splits-like sprawl.

"Oh my God, that was amazing!" Bliss screamed over the music.

I was laughing too hard to answer her.

"Are you okay?" she asked, stepping down.

"Yes," I wheezed.

She sat next to me, and I leaned on her, breathing hard. It was almost a high feeling I had right now, a manic one. Even as I held on to it, I knew it was dangerous.

The fact that I had been sneaking out to have sex with random guys in a house a few blocks over was too much to obsess over in addition to, *Does Tristen like me or not?* So, I wouldn't think about it. I would pretend my sanity wasn't balancing on a knife's edge.

As Bliss and I lay on the floor, my head on her stomach, both of us breathing deep, I almost told her. I even opened my mouth to begin.

But the music set the wrong vibe for that kind of conversation. Or at least, that's what I told myself.

"Let's go sledding."

She pushed me off her stomach and raised herself up onto her elbows. "What is up with you lately? Polar Plunge, dirty dancing, and now sledding? I mean, I guess the sledding isn't that weird, but it's like you're a different person all of a sudden. Normally, I have to drag you to stuff."

I stood up.

"Don't get me wrong," she said, accepting my hand as I pulled her to her feet. "It's awesome. It's like you're the person you've always wanted to be or some shit. But I'm also kind of, like … worried about you."

I picked at my nails, avoiding direct eye contact.

"Is this a Tristen thing? A Brayan thing? I don't get it."

Finally, I raised my gaze to hers. "Maybe it's a Mackenzie thing."

She nodded slowly. "Okay."

I could tell this wasn't the end of it. I was never any good with secrets. She'd find out sooner or later.

"Let's just go sledding." I forced my lips back into a smile. "It will be fun, and we haven't used those saucers we bought."

"I'll see if Tony will drive us," she said. "But you have to feed me first."

"Deal."

The only hill near us that would be any fun was off campus. I'd forgotten about that. And with Tony came Tristen.

After peanut butter sandwiches and Doritos, I pawed through my clothes to try to piece together a sledding outfit. I had a puffy coat and a knit hat and mittens, so that left my legs. I settled on wind pants over jeans.

Tony agreed to take us, and we went to pick up both him and Tristen from their room. My fingers itched inside my mittens as Bliss rapped on their door. Maybe sledding was kind of childish. Maybe Tristen was only going to even the numbers.

Oh God, what if he thinks it's totally lame?

When their door swung open, Tristen was wearing his wool coat I had noticed when he walked me back from Econ but now, there was the addition of fitted ski pants, gloves, and a hat with adorable ear flaps. Both the guys were holding cafeteria trays.

"You can't be serious!" Bliss snorted.

"What? We don't have sleds!" Tony defended. "We greased these babies with Vaseline. If it doesn't work, we'll just jump on with you two." He wiggled his eyebrows at Bliss.

Her face went red as she glanced at the floor.

I pressed my lips together as I tried to contain my laughter. Since when was Bliss shy? Ever?

Tristen cleared his throat. "We gonna do this?"

"Hell yeah!" I cheered, holding up my flimsy blue sled and almost whacking him in the head with it.

"Easy, killer," he said as he helped me lower it.

Our eyes met when his gloved hand brushed my mitten. Even with layers between us, it was dangerously close. Warm. My hands itched again.

The car ride was filled with Bliss's chatter, some of which she aimed at me. I replied in all the right places but didn't say much. Tony's car was small. Small enough that we had to bungee the sleds into the open trunk to drive to the big sledding hill nearby. Small enough that he and Bliss had to tilt their seats forward for Tristen and me to climb into the back.

Small enough that his knee pressed against mine.

Should I move my leg away from his? No, that would make him think I didn't like him. I snuck a glance at him before returning my attention to Bliss. He looked out the window. He probably didn't notice we were touching. Why was I being so psycho about his leg?

He shifted in his seat, and more of his thigh brushed against mine. I was going to have a heart attack.

"We're here!" Bliss yelled.

As soon as Tony was out of the car, I tipped his seat forward, tripping over my feet to get away.

"A little obvious, don't you think?" Bliss hissed in my ear as we walked toward the hill.

Thankfully, Tristen didn't comment.

"Looks kind of dangerous," Tony said as we crested the hill.

He wasn't wrong. There had been so many sledders that half the hill shone with a layer of ice.

"Let's make our own path," Bliss said.

They trudged over to a clearer spot on the hill. Bliss plopped down and began to scoot around on her butt to create a launching space at the top.

I didn't join them. It looked like someone had made a jump at the very end of the slick path. Not a huge one. Just enough that I might be able to catch some air.

I positioned my sled at the top of the iced path and plunked myself down on it, bracing my mittened hands on the hill to keep me in place until I pushed off.

"What the hell are you doing?" Bliss yelled over to me from a dozen yards off, and the boys' heads jerked in my direction.

"I'm sledding!" I replied, smiling.

"You're going to get yourself killed!" She stabbed a mittened hand at me. "Don't be an idiot."

I rolled my eyes. What was the worst thing that could happen? It was sledding. Five-year-olds did this crap.

I pushed off.

The frigid wind whipped over my face, freezing my nose.

As the hill tilted more, my sled started to skid sideways, and I concentrated on keeping myself centered. I gripped the handles so tightly that they dug into my hands despite my thick mittens. The ride was exhilarating, and I laughed out loud, the sound lost behind me.

When I hit the jump, it was like I was moving in slow motion. The sled wrenched off the earth, and I was airborne. This hadn't looked as high from the top of the hill. Oh God, Bliss was right. I was going to get myself killed. Frozen in terror, I clung to the sled like a leech to a bloody wound as it started to drop.

I thought I heard Bliss scream, but it could've been me.

The glazed ground was hard as a rock when I hit it, and no amount of grip strength would have kept me on that sled. The jolt knocked me loose, careening me sideways off the saucer, all limbs and puffy winter coat. My head jerked back to smash against the ice of the hill.

My chest burned as I struggled for air, and my head hurt so bad that my hand flew up to touch it as I rolled to my back.

A cussing Bliss raced to me as fast as her short little legs could in over a foot of snow.

My lungs pulled in the crisp air, puffing it back out in a steamy cloud. My first reaction wasn't to cry over my head, which throbbed something terrible. It was to laugh.

What a dumbass thing to do on the steepest sledding hill in the county.

By the time Bliss made it to me with Tristen and Tony in tow, I was giggling as I stared up at the sunless, overcast sky.

Tristen's concerned face bobbed into my line of vision, blocking out the gray sky. Even with his eyebrows drawn together like that and his cheeks all red, he was still one of the most beautiful men I'd ever seen. He was so my type.

"Hi," I said.

"Hi, crazy girl," he said softly.

The snow crunched as he leaned over me. His mittened hands pushed under my head, and he supported me as I sat up. If it didn't hurt so much, I would probably swoon. Wait, maybe I was swooning. My head had that sloshy feeling. Not good.

"What in the actual fuck, Mackenzie?" Bliss yelled at me.

I winced.

Tristen offered me a hand. He maybe held on to me a little too long, but also maybe not.

I avoided meeting his gaze by searching around in the snow for my hat, which had fallen off in my mad dash. My ears were cold. My wind pants were soaked through, and I shivered a little.

"It looked fun," I said, lifting one shoulder when Bliss continued to glare at me.

"*It looked fun,*" Bliss mimicked in a snotty voice. "What is wrong with you lately?"

"I don't know what you're talking about," I mumbled as she stomped back up the hill, dragging Tony behind her.

I followed along in her wake, Tristen falling in step beside me.

"That was kind of reckless." He said it almost like an apology.

"Maybe I'm a little reckless then."

He frowned at the snow we were stomping through. "It doesn't really fit."

A sharp pain sliced through the back of my head as I shook it. He didn't know me. Lift boot, place, push. It took a lot of effort in this much snow.

"Maybe I don't fit," I said, trying to put distance between us. Physically and emotionally. *I don't fit with you because I'm fucking other men.* There was no way I was actually going to say that.

"Maybe I don't want you to," he said.

I had no response for that.

Because of Bliss's ongoing harassment of my poor choice and the headache that radiated from the back of my head, I kept to the safe path that she and Tony had carved out after that. We slid down the hill a few times before I started shivering, my pants woefully inadequate.

Our initial attempt at having fun was mostly gone anyway, what with everyone asking me about my head every two seconds.

There were only so many times I could say, "I'm okay," when they obviously didn't believe me.

The drive back to the dorm was a silent one. Tristen's knee stayed safely on his side, and I drew my own legs to my side.

Why would I ruin an activity that had been my idea in the first place? I could have solved it with a few funny remarks, but I didn't have it in me.

When I peeled back my pants at the dorm, one layer after another, my legs were a bright, bright red. I almost screamed when the heat of the shower hit them, cursing myself all over again for my stupid idea. But eventually, the blistering heat of the water warmed me up. Even my headache seemed to abate. And everything seemed a little bit less intense. It was sledding, for God's sake. Bliss could chill. I was brave Polar Plunge girl now. She'd just have to adapt.

And Tristen … he'd have to be a friend for now. I was nowhere near done with the house on Maple, and I only had a few hours until I needed to select another door in The Hall of Art and Pleasure.

11

ARE. YOU. READY?

That night, I skipped a door in The Hall of Art and Pleasure. Confidence oozed from my heeled boots as they clicked over the hardwood floor. I touched the paper hanging from the door. I was going to do it, whatever it said. It didn't matter what it was.

Excerpt from "A Woman Waits for Me"
by Walt Whitman

I press with slow rude muscle,
I brace myself effectually, I listen to no entreaties,
I dare not withdraw

I stood there for a moment, my cold hand frozen on the handle of the door. Okay, that was intense. But hadn't I loved the way I was crushed against the padded wall last time, my body responding as the nameless, faceless man pounded into me from behind?

Hadn't I loved the power play of the boxing match, fighting for the first orgasm on the mat?

Hadn't I loved watching myself be fucked in the mirror?

And sure, this was obviously going to go to another level. It might be rougher. The poem wasn't exactly clear.

But that brave, reckless feeling that had permeated the day persisted. And if I was honest with myself, I was angry. I didn't want to identify the reason, but I felt a little like doing something naughty. Naughtier than what I'd already done.

I let out a throaty chuckle that echoed in the long hallway of the house. What was naughtier than returning each night to fuck a new dude?

"I listen to no entreaties …"

No one was watching as my hand fluttered to my breast and pulled at my own nipple sharply. Would it hurt like this? More?

Pain made me uncomfortable, but maybe I could handle it. I would handle it. I wasn't sure what kind of confidence this was supposed to inspire, but at the very least, the rooms in this house were making me brave, making me start to love my body in a completely new way.

I twisted the doorknob and entered the room, immediately stepping through a wall of heat. There was almost a wet quality to it, like a sauna or something. Then my ears detected what my eyes saw a millisecond later—a frothing, bubbling hot tub in the corner.

There was no table, no plaque, no business card telling me what I should do.

That hot tub sure was appealing, especially after the cold of sledding earlier. I peeled back my coat and took off my hat, shaking out my hair for the second time today. There was a hook to the right of the door, and I hung the garments there, then shed my boots and neatly pushed them underneath.

Still no one.

I wasn't going to ignore a steaming hot tub in January. I pulled my clothes off until I wore only my bra and underwear. By the time I turned back to the tub, a shirtless man was there, stepping into the water himself, wearing a pair of black swim trunks. He was on the thinner side, but there was something about him. It was almost like … power? Maybe that was me transferring the poem to him.

I stood on the lip of the hot tub and stared at him as he made himself comfortable in the water. He didn't acknowledge my presence at all. Okay then.

"Hi." I smiled.

He arched a dark eyebrow from where he sat in the frothing water.

Maybe he didn't care whether I joined him or not. I tried not to be offended by that. The tub was where I was headed anyway, so I would get in. Thank God my black panties and bra actually matched.

Where did they find these insanely attractive men? I hated to think that he was getting paid for what we were doing. I liked to think that maybe he wanted this, too. Wanted … me. But I didn't ask, and the silence stretched between us, broken only by the bubbling of the hot tub.

I sighed in contentment as I sank into the water. It was hot. Almost scalding after being out in the winter wind as I walked across campus to this place. Still, it afforded me a little more modesty, and no matter how brave I thought I was, the poem still floated between us.

I listen to no entreaties. I dare not withdraw.

The man hadn't spoken, but I knew as soon as he did—if he did—it would be his voice I'd match to the words of the poem.

I chanced a glance his way. His arms were stretched out, braced on the sides of the tub. His head was thrown back, relaxed, and his eyes were closed. I drifted to the opposite side of the tub and tried to be as relaxed as I knew he was.

Long minutes stretched between us.

Eventually, I closed my eyes, too.

The jets of water kneaded my muscles, and the white noise of the tub lulled me into a place of almost relaxation.

Time passed.

"Are you ready?" he asked.

My eyes flew open, and I regarded him with no little amount of excitement, trying to hide my apprehension.

I listen to no entreaties.

He smiled, his teeth the blinding white of a practiced predator. His hair curled around his face, and I was reminded of an angel in a Renaissance painting. His arms relinquished their position against the edge of the tub, muscles rippling under his skin.

"Are. You. Ready?" This time, he didn't wait for my answer as he stalked me across the large hot tub. There were only three feet between us and his blinding blue eyes now. Two. One.

My chest heaved, and he peered down at my wet breasts, his mouth quirking up when I folded my arms over the shadows of my nipples against the too-thin fabric.

"You only have to say stop," he said, his eyes flickering back to mine, his expression serious. "And I will."

"But it will end then. The rooms will be over," I said breathlessly.

His mouth curled into a wry smile. "Yes."

I sucked in a breath, but I'd already made my decision. "I'm ready."

"You are," he said and closed the distance between us, pressing his chest to mine.

I tilted my head to kiss him, but he chuckled.

"Not yet." He braced his hands on the side of the tub and jumped out of the water.

"Come on," he said to me, holding his hand out to help me up.

"I prefer the stairs," I said, suddenly shy.

I backed off to where they were located, and he sighed.

"You're not very obedient, are you?" he asked nonchalantly, using a towel from a nearby chair to dry off.

I thought about it for half a second. "Why would I be?"

He barked out another laugh.

"Well, I'm sorry," I huffed as I climbed the stairs and immediately grabbed a towel, wrapping it around my body, a thick shield between us. "I'm not exactly accustomed to whatever it is you want," I said in a snarky voice.

He threw his towel to the side. "Are you taking a tone with me?"

I could have easily said no. Part of me knew I was taunting him on purpose, wanting to know what would happen if I pushed him too far.

"And if I am?"

His eyes followed my tongue as it flicked out to lick my lips.

"Drop the towel," he commanded.

"No," I said, backing away from him and the tub. "And what are you going to do about it?" I singsonged as I stumbled back.

He growled and caught up to me, yanking the towel away. "I think you *want* to be punished."

My breath caught in my throat. *Punished how?*

"Do you?" His voice was hard, almost cruel.

"Do I what?" I asked, still playing the part of the bitchy girl.

"Want to be punished?" His rough hands skated down my arms until they circled my wrists. He wasn't much taller than me, but wiry muscles flexed under the skin of his arms.

I shivered. "Maybe," I whispered.

"Good," he said and held my wrists as he backed up. When his knees hit the side of a sofa in the corner, he sat.

Part of me—the part that wasn't in the moment right now—balked at the fact that he was wearing wet swim trunks and sitting on the sofa. He was going to ruin it! The other part of me realized that he still held my wrists in a firm vise.

He jerked me down until I fell. He caught me, twisting me across his lap, my rear end in the air.

I moved to get off his lap, and he chuckled.

"It will be worse if you struggle," he warned.

Wait, what? No. There's no way. My cheeks flamed, and I wiggled against him, trying to escape.

He sighed, his arm tightening around me.

"I really, really wouldn't," he whispered, his voice threatening in my ear.

I stilled. I was teasing, for pity's sake. I didn't think he was really going to physically punish me!

Maybe I wasn't ready for this.

His hand slid over my panties, pulling the sides up until they were trapped between my ass cheeks, leaving them bare. His fingers moved over the freshly exposed skin once, twice, three times.

Okay, maybe I was wrong. This wasn't so bad. It was actually kind of calming. My muscles relaxed beneath his firm grip.

When his palm came down on my ass the first time, it was almost playful. I barely felt it.

"See how gentle I can be?" he crooned. "You really should've done what you were told."

When his hand came down a second time, it was much sharper, and my body jerked in response.

Ow!

But as soon as the slap was over, he kneaded my ass, massaging away the hurt. I shifted on his lap when his erection pressed against my side.

"Three more," he said as his hand came down again. This time, it was even harder.

I almost cried out, but I bit my lip. My nipples tightened as the massaging began again. I couldn't see anything through my curtain of hair, and the blood was rushing to my head. Really, that was probably enough. He'd made his point.

"God, your ass is so round," he groaned. "I'm going to make it pink as fuck."

I didn't even have time to react to his words before he switched sides on the next slap, the sound of his hand meeting my ass louder than the bubbling of the hot tub in the corner. My breath got caught in my throat, a small gasp escaping me.

"Why are you fighting your reaction?" he asked, bending over until he was near the hair that fell over my ear. His silky voice made goosebumps spread from my neck down to my shoulders. "I want to hear you scream. You seem the type."

What an ass. I bucked in anger, trying to throw him off, but he held me fast.

"Feisty," he teased.

"You don't know anything about me."

"You're clenching." He chuckled.

With my breasts pressed against his knees and my scalp starting to tingle, I kind of wanted to hit *him*.

Just get it over with, I wanted to say, but I didn't struggle.

As he had said, it would only make it worse.

"It's kind of a challenge," he taunted. "And you were such a brat to me," he said. Then he paused. "Remember, you only have to say stop."

Like hell I would.

When his hand came down the last time, it was harder than the rest, and God help me, I let out a small yelp of pain.

Dammit.

"Oh, baby. I knew you were a loud one," he said, letting go of me.

I scrambled off his lap. My chest was heaving, and I knew my face was red from being upside down. As I stood before him in nothing but scrunched-up underwear and a see-through bra, I was incensed at him winning. I was also embarrassed. This man had been inches from my naked ass, and it was fully lit in this part of the room. I breathed hard for a second, angry and confused and exposed. I balled my hands into fists.

His smile turned dangerous. "You wanna try it? I dare you."

I launched myself at him, not really knowing what it was I wanted. Maybe to scratch out his eyes. How dare he make me feel like I was in trouble! How dare he overpower me! But did I want him? Hell yes, I did. What we did was so erotic that even though shame coursed through me, it was also spiked with a heat I didn't quite understand.

Even as we fought, the wetness gathered between my thighs.

The hot tub, I told myself, but it sounded weak, even in my own head.

He tackled me to the couch and pinned my arms above my head. When he used his knee to separate my legs, a tingle ran through me, and I had to admit it.

I was turned on. Turned on big time.

Motherfucker.

He transferred both my wrists to one of his hands, still holding me in place, and used the other to reach down and touch me.

"Babe," he said almost gently, "you're soaked."

I jerked against him, my nipples brushing against his chest through the thin fabric of my bra. I let go of a breath, arching my back even more, my breasts aching for the stimulation.

"I'm going to let you go, Mackenzie. And you know what you're going to do for me?"

I tilted my head.

"You're going to take off those sexy black panties and let me fuck you."

My stomach clenched at his words. He was such a dick, but I wanted nothing more than for him to claim me, to make me scream in pleasure.

He groaned. "You have no idea how much you're turning me on right now."

When he released me, I wasted no time in shimmying out of my underwear, dropping it unceremoniously to the floor.

He shed his shorts casually, laid them over the side of a nearby chair, then turned to me with a condom in his hand.

Whoa. Talk about a thick cock.

He slid the condom on with one hand. His head dipped, and he caught one of my nipples between his teeth through my bra, giving me what I needed.

"Oh God," I gasped. The burn of his mouth on me was so deliciously wrong.

"I knew you could be a good girl," he crooned.

Then he was on top of me, pushing me back into the cushions, and his dick was at my entrance. Solid and wide, he nudged at me, and I froze. Too big. There was such a thing as too big.

"Shh," he said, pinching my nipple with one hand while the other found my clit. "You can handle it."

Then inch by slow inch, he entered me, stretching me as far as I could go. I let out a whimper, but his mouth came down on mine, tasting me. I wanted him in me, but I didn't know how it would work.

When he reached the deepest part of me, he started to withdraw. Again, it was so slow, and I could feel my body trying to adapt. We continued that way—slow, steady, safe—but I knew I couldn't get off this way. Not today. Not even with his hand expertly touching the most sensitive place. I arched against him, biting his lip.

More.

All hell broke loose. He began a relentless rhythm, in and out, push and push and push.

"Oh fuck," he said, his body rising until he was almost completely out of me, then slamming all the way back in. It was jarring, teeth-rattling, borderline painful.

I loved it.

His mouth switched to my other breast, and he rolled my nipple between his teeth.

The waves of my orgasm began, like water lapping at a beach before a storm.

He stopped, halfway in me.

"Not until I tell you to," he said roughly.

"What?" The ripples of my orgasm faded away.

"You don't get to come yet."

"What the fuck?"

111

I struggled under him, but he didn't let me go.

He started rubbing my clit with expert fingers, but that wasn't the kind of orgasm I'd been close to.

"I need …" The words escaped me before I could call them back.

"Yes?" he asked, a challenge in that one word that I couldn't back down from.

I moaned. My head fell back against the couch cushion. "Fuck you," I panted.

A different kind of pleasure was building as his fingers swirled around my clit.

"Fuck me, huh?" he asked, his voice teasing, and then he slammed into me again.

"Holy …"

But his fingers didn't stop.

"Fuck *me*?" he asked again as he increased his thrusts, his voice raspy.

"Yeah …" I said, but I couldn't form a coherent thought. I had been so close, and now, I was so … I was so close in a different way, and this … this had never happened to me before.

"Say it," he said.

"Fuck …" I replied.

"Say all of it, and I'll let you come," he said.

He was so presumptuous, but I couldn't think.

I just needed it.

He picked up speed in both his hand and his hips. "Say it."

"Fuck me," I whispered, half in a daze, and he shifted his hips at the same time he flicked my clit.

I screamed as I came, holding on to him for dear life as he continued pumping into me.

He shuddered, his breathing ragged as he came, too.

My whole body clenched, my insides clutching at him as helplessly as my arms were, my nails digging ruthlessly into his back.

The orgasm lasted longer than it ever had before, my body shaking and shifting, pleasure rippling out from my center.

"Oh, babe …" he said, his hand continuing to massage my clit, prolonging the sweet torture, even as he withdrew from me.

But my eyes were closed. I was unable to process any more information. I was a live wire, all nerve and feeling and holy fucking fuck.

When my body finally stopped shaking, he cleared his throat.

"That was"—his eyes were wide when mine flicked open— "really great," he said, expression intense.

But then the lights flicked off, and we both knew what that meant.

"Confidence," he murmured.

I blew out a ragged breath. *Holy shit.*

12

I KNOW YOU

I lay there naked for long moments after. The dark stretched endlessly, my breathing the only thing to break the silence. Someone must've turned the hot tub off. Or maybe it timed out.

Why did I even notice that?

When the lights clicked back on, the room still seemed charged. I changed quickly and got the hell out of Maple House.

I rushed home, the energy from earlier in the day escaping with every step. These men who had sex with me … I hadn't really thought about them as people until today. But when I'd looked into his eyes after we came … the spell had broken.

As I trekked into my hall and over to the elevator, I had a sobering realization—I didn't want the spell to break. I didn't want to think about this as anything other than a fantasy. There was a part of me that didn't even believe it was happening to me. Years from now, I wanted to look back and laugh at how crazy it was.

But now … now, I couldn't do that.

I punched the Up button a little too hard, and my pointer finger cracked. "Ow." I sucked on the knuckle.

It didn't hurt that bad, but in an instant, I was crying. Not a heart-wrenching sob, but a silent grief that came from deep within me and poured down my face.

What was I doing, going to some place called The Hall of Art and Pleasure?

Why had I thought it would solve anything for me? Brayan wouldn't want me back if he knew a bunch of guys had had sex with me. Tristen wouldn't want me if he knew what I was doing. And that guy … the one who dominated me? I would never see him again, and what if we would've been good for each other in real life? What if …

No. Stop it.

I didn't need another relationship so soon after Brayan. I needed time to heal. Or to flirt maybe.

"Confidence," they'd all said.

That was what this was about. Not any of the guys in my life. It was about me.

Other people piled into the elevator, giving me lots of space. I was that crazy crying girl.

But I couldn't stop.

And when I stood in front of my dorm room door, I knew it wasn't where I wanted to be. Bliss would figure out where I'd been. She'd force it out of me. But I didn't have anywhere else to go.

Except …

I walked down the hall to Tristen's room. He wanted to be friends, right? It probably wasn't true, but …

I knocked.

He wouldn't even be there. He'd be out with Tony. Or another girl.

The door opened, and there he was, hair all mussed, wearing sweatpants and a hoodie. Headphones hung loosely around his neck, and when he saw my face, he softened visibly, his eyebrows knitting together with concern.

This was what I needed, whether I deserved it from him or not. I threw myself into his arms and cried.

And he let me.

He led me over to his green futon—a different color than ours, though still the same shitty construction. He wrapped me in the blanket there and turned on the TV, hugging me to his side as I soaked his hoodie with my stupidity.

He surfed for a few minutes, finally clicking on an episode of a mindless, physical game show. We sat in silence as contestant after contestant went up against a curved wall. Eventually, my breathing evened out, and I calmed down, but my chest still hitched with suppressed sobs. I molded myself against him further, hiding my face in his shoulder.

"Wanna talk about it?" His voice was different. Low, serious, husky.

I almost shivered. There was no way in hell I was ever sharing the Maple House secret with him.

"It's dumb. And complicated. Talking won't help." My voice was scratchy. Was I getting a cold? Or was it from crying?

He nodded.

My body relaxed.

He rubbed my arm. Immediately, it sparked something in me.

What the fuck? I was not allowed to be turned on again tonight. This wasn't right. I had to leave.

But then he started a circular rubbing pattern on my back, and it was so soothing that I couldn't have budged if a hundred angry rhinos had plowed into me.

I closed my eyes.

I didn't know how long I was out, but when I woke up, my head was in his lap.

"You snore," he said in a teasing voice.

The game show still played on the TV. His hand was still on my back.

I jerked upright.

"Only when I cry or am sick," I said. "I, um … this—" I gestured to the futon.

He ran his hand through his hair. "Don't read into it," he said, his eyes earnest as he gazed into my swollen ones. "It was no big deal."

He was right. He was so right. And I had no excuse for the way I was using him. I had no right to do anything with him at all. If I'd thought he was too good for me before, this definitely proved it.

I folded the blanket, my face turned away from his. "Thanks for being my person today," I muttered, pushing the folds of the fabric down in a neat little square.

"It's cool," he said, getting up and stretching his arms above his head. Sitting that way with me for so long must have made him stiff. "Anytime."

"Cool." There was nothing else to do but pretend it was okay.

I was ruining everything.

"Out meeting mystery man again?" Bliss asked from her laptop when I carefully shut the door of our dorm. "Or were you with Tristen?"

I was too tired to lie. "Both."

"What? You're kidding!"

She shoved her papers aside but then got a load of my face. I must have looked like total shit.

"Are you okay?" Her voice was kind, but as much as I'd needed that from Tristen was as much as I didn't want it from Bliss.

She was my *tell it like it is* person, the person who held me accountable. And Tristen … he was something different.

"Am I okay?" I repeated, my mouth tasting the question before I lied about it. "Yeah." I sat down next to her on the tiny rectangle of the futon not covered by her homework.

"Look, I know I was kind of an ass about Brayan. I'm really sorry it didn't go the way you wanted it to. Did you love him? Is that what this is all about?"

I rolled my eyes to the ceiling. One single strand of a cobweb floated in the circulated air above us.

"No. I don't know," I told the cobweb. "I don't know what I'm doing anymore."

"Yeah, but isn't that what college is about? Figuring shit out? I think you need to give yourself a break, Kenz. You're just doing what we all are. It's okay to be human."

Yeah, it was okay to be human, but what I was doing, what Tristen meant to me … it wasn't fair or right.

"Mmhmm," I said.

She gave me a look, then opened another textbook.

I should tell her everything, but it was easier to let her get back to studying.

The next morning, I dragged myself to class, blearily stomping through the snow no one had bothered to get rid of for students this morning even though we were still expected to go to classes. It was a good thing I had great boots.

Crunch, crunch, crunch.

It lulled me into a sense of duty, of routine. I dearly needed that today. I watched my feet slip in and out of the white salt stains already splashed across the rubber.

When I looked up again, I was almost at the lecture hall, but my gaze ran straight into another student's. Passing each other on narrow walkways was bound to happen to most of us. It was the familiar set to his jaw that stopped me short.

It was the man from the first room. The one who had fucked me against a mirror. Only now, he was wearing a puffy black coat and a scarf in school colors as he battled the wind.

He goes here? No, that's impossible … isn't it?

His gaze skittered away from mine, and he stepped aside to pass by me. I should do what he was doing. It would kill the fantasy otherwise. But for some reason, I couldn't let him go. I moved to his side of the sidewalk, blocking his path.

"I …" I didn't know what to say.

He attempted to get past me one more time, his hand on the strap of his backpack, but I stepped in front of him again.

"Excuse me," he said politely.

"I know you," I said, catching his eye again.

And though I thought I saw the same flare of recognition in his eyes, it was gone in an instant as he regarded me coolly.

His hands on me, his body against mine as he made me watch myself being fucked. I couldn't forget that. I couldn't forget what we had done.

"No, you don't." He smiled. That same smile.

I am naked first. His arms outstretched.

"Yes, I do," I said, placing one mittened hand on his chest.

He stared at it, and I dropped my hand quickly.

"No"—he looked straight at me— "you don't." He seemed to be trying to tell me something. Something important. His voice had too much weight to it.

I nodded my head slowly, backing away from him. "Sorry," I mumbled. "I must have been mistaken."

"It's no big deal," he said, his voice still cool, still polite. Then he cracked a smile. "Have a great rest of your week."

It was only after he turned the corner that I realized there was a double meaning in his words. *That bastard! He was talking about the rest of the week at Maple House!* I had half a mind to turn around and demand answers from him.

But duty prevailed.

I shook out my hat and placed my gloves on the register at the back of the lecture hall and sank into my regular seat. Ignoring me on campus must be an unspoken rule of the house.

Did they sign up for this? How did a guy even get selected? Was it based on the fantasy they wanted to act out, or whether they were hot, or ...

I giggled as other students filed in, imagining the student fair recruiting guys to have sex with girls on campus. It wouldn't be hard to find any number of men to do that sort of thing. I was so lost in my fantasy that it wasn't long before the lecture was over, and I had no notes.

The walk from class to the dining commons seemed like it took ten years, and then it was time for my next class. I lost myself in the rhythm of my daily routine again. Rinse, repeat, go, go, go until, finally, my phone vibrated with my alarm, and I had to return to The Hall of Art and Pleasure.

13

ARE YOU BRAVE?

I could tell Bliss about where I was going every night.

There wasn't any rule to keep it secret, but I couldn't bring myself to share anything. Not yet anyway. If I told and someone found out, would I be expelled from the house? I couldn't take that risk. I couldn't stop until it was done. I needed to finish it. And there weren't many days left. I wanted to see the test. If this was destructive behavior—if this was something I shouldn't be doing to myself—then it wasn't like it would last much longer.

I hummed with nervous energy as I climbed the stairs to the house on Maple. No matter my mental torment, my body was reacting. This week, it was like all bets were off. My rational brain knew the whole thing was completely strange and unlike anything I should ever be doing.

But my body? It definitely appealed to my body. A tingle of excitement burst inside me as I approached a door in the hall. The sheet of paper hanging from a single nail showed a crudely drawn sketch of a woman bent over a table.

Are you brave?

Brave how? The clues for these rooms were getting more and more vague.

I looked at the doors I'd already visited, the outsides of them now empty of papers. It appeared I couldn't visit a room more than once. I couldn't go back, and the farther I walked down this hallway, the more powerful the fantasies.

I opened the door.

A man was already there, his hands braced on a rectangular table. It was the only piece of furniture in the room, smack dab in the center.

He was entirely naked.

From what I could see, the guy was muscular, but not overly so. He looked about as old as the rest, probably in college, like me. After today, I knew he could be anyone.

What if I sat in the same lecture hall as him? The thought, instead of making me panic, turned me on further. *How did someone my own age get to be so confident? Were they trained in what they would do to me? How did that work?*

I eyed him.

He waited for a long moment, but when I didn't walk over to him, he sighed. "I want to fuck you, but I don't have much time."

"Okay …"

He has plans other than this? Will we end up at the same sports bar I go to with Bliss? Will he pick up another girl and have his way with her tonight, too? Two in one night? God, that must take some stamina. It was kinda dirty. Kinda hot.

"Strip and get your sexy ass on the table." He smacked it, his jaw tense. "Let me have you." His voice was sharp and impatient, and it made me bristle.

My body was crazy attracted to him, but my mind was definitely not.

"I bet you're an asshole in real life," I said in response, even as I disrobed, kicking my clothes away from myself. I couldn't help it. He wasn't exactly being seductive.

He smacked the table again. "Does it matter if I can make you come?"

I was in such a weird, disjointed mood today, and it was kind of a relief to be nasty to someone. All my pent-up frustration over this whole thing, about not being able to talk about it, was rising to the surface. And I wouldn't ever see this man again, right?

"Oh, fuck you," I spat.

"Nah, fuck you. On the table." He slapped it a third time.

I folded my arms.

He chuckled. "Is this doing it for you, sweetheart?"

Was I turned on? Not really. I lifted one shoulder and let it drop, and he pressed his lips together, his disappointment evident.

"You need me to be sweet today." He sounded let down.

His eyes were an intense green. I hadn't seen that from across the room. Was he wearing contacts?

I hopped on the table without looking at him. "I don't need anything from you."

His hand reached up and tilted my chin until I was forced to stare at him. He studied me for a long moment. Then his head dipped, and he sucked hard on my exposed left breast. I gasped.

"I can be your distraction, Mackenzie," he murmured, his hot breath stimulating my now-wet nipple.

I shivered. The fact that the men knew my name hadn't escaped me, but, God, it was so sexy and personal when they said it. Like they actually cared about my pleasure.

His hand reached forward until curled around the small of my back, his mouth sucking until it was almost painful. Then he stopped, immediately capturing my other nipple with his teeth.

My breath hitched.

He smiled up at me. "Let me introduce you to something new." His fingers pinched my nipple sharply.

"Something new?" I gasped, reveling in the bolt of painful pleasure that zigzagged through me at his touch.

"Like this," he said, twisting my nipple slightly before letting go. "But different. Are you brave?" he asked, echoing the paper on the door.

I nodded, though I wasn't really sure I was.

"Let's start with what you think you want right now," he said, and with that, he pulled me off the table, bending me over it face-first until my cheek pressed against the now-warmed wood, like the girl in the picture. "Hold the sides," he ordered.

I did as he said.

Then he pushed his face against me from behind.

I bucked against the wood, trying to shimmy away. "What are you doing?" I cried.

He reached up and captured my hips with his hands, his tongue reaching into my folds from behind, licking, probing, sucking.

"Fuck, your ass is hot," he groaned against me.

Then as fast as he had begun his onslaught, it was gone.

"Fuck," he said again, spreading my cheeks wide. Then he pushed into me hard.

He was long, and his strokes were powerful as he fucked me, but I was in a destructive mood. An angry one still. It wasn't enough to make me come.

He pulled out before he came, shooting his load into the condom. Then he tossed it into a trash can at the side of the room.

Ready for the lights to dim, I started to close my legs. *Well, that was disappointing.*

"Where are you going?" he asked as I moved to get up from the table.

"What?" I asked.

"On your knees, Mackenzie."

"On my ..."

When I turned, he held his flaccid manhood in one fist.

"On your knees."

It was then that I realized what he wanted. Ugh. It made total sense. Didn't all douchebags want girls to suck them off? Despite my shit mood and my annoyance with it all today, I dropped to my knees and took him into my mouth. His dick began to harden as his hands pulled back my curls. Then he smiled and began to fuck my mouth.

He never went too hard, and he never gagged me, but his dick thrust in and out in a savage rhythm while his hands threaded through my curls to hold my head in place. I couldn't have protested if I'd wanted to. I could feel him growing inside my mouth, my submission probably giving him as much pleasure as the blow job itself. I relaxed my jaw. He jammed inside, so close to choking me that I fully expected it to happen. My hand drifted down to touch where he'd tasted earlier. I should at least be getting some pleasure out of all of this. I moaned as I stroked my clit, the vibration of my throat against his dick making it even harder.

I'd never been much for wanting to give a blow job since I was so inexperienced, but this guy took all the guesswork out of it, and for that, I was grateful. He fucked my mouth the exact way he wanted to, and I knew he was enjoying himself from the rock-hard situation happening again so quickly after he came. It lasted for all of a minute before he let me go.

"Assume the same position as before," he told me, his cock dripping with my spit and hard as fuck.

I blinked up at him. *We aren't going to finish?* I'd been revving myself up to. *Is he going to do … that thing … he did again? Eating me out from behind?*

I turned back around, subjecting my breasts once again to the polished wood of the table.

His hand found my pussy, and he slowly inserted two fingers. I was still wet from being fucked a few moments prior, and I felt it when those fingers drifted up to my asshole.

Is he going to …

His finger pushed against that place, meeting the resistance with determination until he was knuckle deep. The pressure made me gasp as I remembered the boxing room. Not quite painful, but not quite pleasurable either. Full. Different. Weird?

"I have lube," he said. "And a really fun toy. Are you brave?" he asked for the second time.

I hesitated. He was such an asshole. I was in a bad mood. But there was something else lurking underneath those emotions, simmering beneath the surface. Was I brave? Maybe I wouldn't call it that, but I was something. As exposed as I was to him now, it didn't make me shy. What did I have to be embarrassed about if he was the one who wanted my ass?

"I'm brave," I whispered, my face blazing.

He slapped one of my exposed cheeks. "This is going to be fun. Stay there. Hold the sides of the table."

I did, but I couldn't help my body from shaking a little. I was nervous. I heard his chuckle from behind me.

There was a cold sensation as something was poured down my crack. His fingers immediately followed, and he pushed into my pussy again, kneading my ass cheek in time with his motion. My breathing became quicker as he went deeper and deeper, touching my inner walls in swirling motions that drove me wild. I was close to coming when his fingers withdrew.

More of the cold. This time, a finger inserted into my ass, meeting that same resistance, foreign and a little uncomfortable again. That alone was exciting. The prospect of doing something new with him, something I'd always thought was completely taboo … it was so hot.

"You are so fucking tight," he whispered brokenly. "I want it. I want that ass."

I heard a buzzing from behind me and almost backed off the table in surprise, but he used one hand to hold my face down against the table.

A slim shaft slid into my vagina, another part resting against my clit, and I cried out at the intense vibration emanating from it.

He turned down the vibration, and my body still climbed toward my inevitable orgasm, but less quickly.

"Ooh," I moaned.

"Are you brave?" he replied.

I nodded against the wood again, hardly trusting myself to speak.

He held my ass cheeks apart, positioning himself at my entrance.

"Relax, baby." He rocked into my ass an inch, maybe two.

I reached back in half-hearted protest at the intense pressure, but he didn't relent. Inch by slow, torturous, lubed inch, he worked his way into me.

"Ooh," I moaned.

His cock inside me, stretching me this way, felt so strange, so different. Weirdly satisfying. He stayed fully seated a moment, and my body adapted, my brain once again focused on the toy providing me with pleasure. Then the vibration increased as he slowly withdrew himself. The feeling of him leaving my ass, combined with the intense sensation on my clit, made me shudder, but then he was back, stretching me, hurting me just a little.

He established a slow rhythm. In. Pause. Let me climb. Out. I almost come. Back in and start over.

Slowly, he built up speed, and he turned the vibrator up again. I started to relax a little more as he thrust in and out. Soon, I was arching to meet him on his reentry as his hand palmed the flesh of my left cheek. My breasts pressed against the wood as I gripped the edges of the table with my fingernails.

"Just fuck me," I gasped, wanting more. Needing an end to this, in one way or another, either by pain or by pleasure. I needed something.

"No," he said, gritting his teeth in concentration.

For a moment, I was confused by it. Then it dawned on me. Despite his appearance, despite the asshole he presented himself as, he was trying not to hurt me.

"Be a douche and just do it," I said. "It's the only way I'll come." I wasn't sure whether that was right or not, but I didn't care anymore. This was torture. I'd been too close for too long.

He paused for a second, and then the vibrator ratcheted to an intense vibration that echoed in the room like the buzzing of angry bees. It took away my breath.

OhmyGod, ohmyGod, ohmyGod. It was going to make me come.

Then he started slamming into me from behind, his dick rushing in and out of my ass the same way he'd pounded my pussy only minutes earlier. I was determined to take it all, the pressure and release both welcome and overwhelming.

"Oh fuck!" he shouted into the near silence of the room.

I was breathing hard, moaning.

"Yeah, Mackenzie!" he yelled.

I arched my back even more and thrust my ass up, needing this. Needing more.

"Holy shit," he said.

His dick thrust harder into me, and the ripples of my orgasm began. The waves started low but magnified with every thrust.

"Ah, babe." He shuddered, his body collapsing on top of me, even as I whimpered with the force of the orgasm that was still unfurling inside me.

"You are brave," he panted, slipping out of me.

He grabbed the remote from the table, and the vibrations stopped. He pulled the toy out of me, the absence of it both a relief and a disappointment.

"Confidence," he said, slapping my butt lightly.

The lights went out, and his footsteps faded.

I unfolded myself from my place on the table, but when I turned around, I wasn't surprised that he was gone.

And my ass was fucking sore.

14

GAME ON

I shoved my hands in my pockets and power-walked through snow that thickened by the minute. That session had been … intense. Hate fucking was something I'd read about, seen in movies, but never experienced. And sure, the guy at Maple House and I hadn't hated each other for real, but it was close enough. My chest was lighter. It had been like an exorcism or something.

When I walked into our room, Bliss eyed my hair, covered in white snowflakes and wild from being smashed against the table in The Hall of Art and Pleasure. Her gaze swept over my wrinkled clothes and the heat in my cheeks.

"You just had sex," she accused.

"So?"

She didn't need to know everything, but I didn't feel like hiding everything from her either.

"But Tristen is in his room. And you weren't there?"

"Nope." I fished in our mini fridge for a Diet Pepsi. I popped it open and sat on the futon with her, draping my legs over her lap.

"I thought you liked him," she said quietly.

It was only a matter of time before she got fed up with my half-answers. Honestly, she'd held out longer than I thought she would.

"I do like him," I admitted reluctantly. "Probably more than I should."

"So, you're out having sex with someone else?" She nodded, as if this made sense.

My eyes skittered away from where she sat. "Do you want to watch something?" I asked, reaching backward to grab the remote from the side table. Maybe if I changed the subject, she'd get the hint.

"Are you going out every night to screw some stranger …" Her eyes strayed to the open door.

I stood up and closed it, which was all the confirmation she needed.

"Did Brayan hurt you that bad? What's happening here?"

All I could think to say was, "It's not like that." I traced a pattern in the wood of the door. Knots upon knots.

"Are you in love with this new guy?"

"No."

My answer was so swift that she reeled back.

"Who are you, and what did you do with Mackenzie?"

I turned and shook my head at the shag carpet rug we'd bought together two weeks ago. We'd been tired of cold feet and slipping around on our socks on the concrete floor of the common room. I spied a piece of lint on it. We should probably vacuum.

Finally, finally, finally, I lifted my eyes. *Confidence.* If I couldn't tell her all of it, she could still hear part of the truth. The part I was proud of.

"That Mackenzie doesn't exist anymore." As I said it, I realized that every word was true. I wasn't in love with these men.

She snapped her laptop shut and retreated to her side of the room.

Whatever.

She wanted me to be less attached, didn't she? That was what the whole strip-club adventure had been about, hadn't it? I was just following her original orders. She couldn't be mad at me for that. And if she was, that was her problem.

After a blistering hot shower, I plugged my earbuds into my phone and lay, staring at the stupid glow-in-the-dark star I'd placed on the ceiling. Just the one because it had been too much effort to finish the job. I needed to close out my week in The Hall of Art and Pleasure. There were too many unfinished things around me already. Bliss could wait for an explanation until then.

I hoped.

Waking up the next morning was especially hard, so I decided to play hooky from all my responsibilities. I wouldn't go to any lectures or to the library to study. I wouldn't hang out with anyone. I just wanted to be alone.

But after a few hours of flipping through a novel and surfing social media, I realized that doing nothing was actually making everything worse. I needed out, away from the sex and Tristen and even Bliss.

When the best idea ever wiggled its way into my brain, I could have smacked myself for not thinking of it sooner. I was an adult now! I could take an actual vacation. For one day anyway. There was an indoor water park south of town and a bus stop on campus that would take me directly there. There was a student rate, so it wouldn't ruin me financially.

I was going to hang out in the lazy river on a raft; sip some strawberry daiquiris procured with my fake ID; and relax in the hot tub. It was going to be glorious.

I slipped my Polar Plunge bikini on under my sweats and threw my hair into a messy bun.

With no makeup and no real plan, I boarded the bus two dorms past mine in flip-flops and a winter coat.

It was exactly what I needed. When I pushed through the door and into the wet heat of the water park, I wasn't sad that I didn't have Bliss with me, or Tristen, or anyone else. I was able to set my own schedule, free from anyone else's expectations of a good time. Life could be so narrow in the dorms, everyone on top of each other. I'd forgotten what it was like to actually breathe a little bit.

I ordered my daiquiri and created a routine. Drink on a lounge chair or in the sauna; go down the lazy river, trailing my fingers along the water; then get all warm and comfy in the hot tub until the temperature became too much.

It was pretty busy because it was the dead of winter, but the people around me were all absorbed with their own families. I didn't have to speak at all. The bartender figured out what I wanted after the first two drinks, so all I had to do was bring her my empty.

Hours passed, and I kept myself on the edge of tipsy and drunk the whole time, ordering nachos and ice cream and not even caring about the stomachache it would cause after the mostly clean eating that Bliss and I normally stuck to. I needed grease the way I needed this day to recharge.

Eventually, I would have to face everything. The schoolwork I was missing, Bliss's anger, Tristen's confusion. The house. By the time I allowed myself to think about any of it, shivering in the cold at the bus stop as I waited in the dark for the last run, none of it seemed that dramatic anymore.

I would finish my stint at the house, and then I could be with Tristen. Then I'd tell Bliss about it, and she'd understand. It would all be fine.

Bliss wasn't home when I got there, and I went into a bit of a sneezing fit while I got changed, so it was just as well. She was a total germ freak. Even a little cold would make her sanitize the entire dorm.

Then back into the cold I went, stomping out the bonelessness of the water park. Without much thought, I climbed the old steps to the house on Maple and entered. Soon, I stood in front of the next room, the snow on my boots melting into a puddle at my feet.

I studied the tag on the new door, having trouble registering what I was supposed to do.

It's not like any of these read like an instruction manual anyway, so it's okay, I told myself.

I'd just do what it said. Have sex. Go back to my dorm. Repeat.

I was recharged and ready for whatever. What was I supposed to be learning from this place again? All the different ways to orgasm?

Confidence.

My eyes scanned the paper. It was pixelated, like one of those old video games, with one short message on it.

Please wait. System loading …

Well, sure. Whatever that meant. Wait. Those weren't pixels. It was a collage. I stepped closer until my nose almost bumped against the paper. It was a collage of people having sex, each image so tiny that I could barely tell in the low light what they were doing.

The Hall of *Art* and *Pleasure* indeed.

I squared my shoulders as I twisted the knob.

The room was dark when I entered, except for a glow from a mid-sized flat screen. Some sort of first-person shooter game was displayed on it. From behind the couch, I could dimly see a shaggy-haired head facing the TV.

I walked forward, still hugging my coat to me. When I was level with the couch, I watched as the character on the screen shot someone else, then glanced at the guy playing. He was slouched over, wearing a pair of basketball shorts and an oversize hoodie. There was stubble on his cheeks, and he was wearing a headset that he occasionally chuckled into. With his sloppy hair, he was every bit the opposite of my normal type. I liked clean-cut men, men with overt muscles. Basically, an ROTC recruit was a wet dream to me.

Still, as I watched his fingers move over the controller, the way he swore colorfully into the headset, how he flipped his hair out of his face, I was a little attracted to the amount of focus he had. Kind of wanted to break it.

When I'd first seen the sign, I'd thought that it seemed a bit tame, a bit odd compared to what I'd already experienced on the, um … table.

Am I supposed to play the video game with him?

Or … maybe I'm supposed to seduce him?

I was out of my depth with no direction. *How do I even begin? And doesn't he know that we're going to have sex anyway? Otherwise, why is he here, in this room?*

I could make the first move at least. "Hi."

He didn't look up but used his controller to pull out a knife and shank someone, even as part of his screen went red as he was shot once. It faded away a moment later, and he made his character run to a new location.

"Hi," he said, distracted and much later than I would have liked. "Just point and wait. No, it's not worth it. Get there."

I had no idea what he was talking about, but video games didn't interest me much.

"What are you playing?" I asked as I gingerly sat on the couch next to him. No other controller was in sight.

He didn't answer me.

"The fucking sniper, man! How did you miss him? Jesus, do I have to do everything by myself?" He fired off another round of shots on the controller.

I noticed the way his lean fingers pushed against the buttons and had the odd thought that I'd like his thumb inside me. He moved it rather well.

I stood and walked around the arm of the couch, passing between him and the screen. He tilted his body to look around me. I sat next to him again. He was talking to someone on the other side of the headset.

"Go to the rendezvous point and don't fuck anything else up."

Okay then. I moved my hand to his thigh, and he flinched a little as he continued to play. It was enough to give me a modicum of confidence, but that was all I needed. I inched my hand up and inward.

It was easy to see that he was concentrating hard on the game, but it was just as obvious that he was distracted by my touch. I pulled my hair back into the rubber band that lived on my wrist. Frizzy hair in the summer, voluminous curls in the winter. It was my life.

I knew what I wanted to do before I attempted it, but would he be a willing participant? What was I thinking? Of course he would.

He was in the room, wasn't he? I had a feeling this was exactly what this room was about. Me seducing a gamer on the couch.

I sank to my knees in front of him and parted his legs. *Confidence.*

15

CROSSING THE LINE

The gamer continued to press the buttons on his controller, but he didn't say anything to the other players.

I reached forward to pull down his shorts and boxers a few inches but met resistance. He was already hard.

He cleared his throat, and I looked up at him, but he quickly averted his eyes back to the screen before I had the chance to say anything. So, that was the game.

I definitely got to be in charge. I got to make him want to fuck me.

Well, I was going to have a little fun first. Pulling his manhood out of his shorts, I appreciated the weight of him for a moment before slipping its entirety in my mouth.

His fingers stilled on the controller. His character was immediately hit.

"What the hell, dude? It was an easy shot!" I heard faintly from his headset, and I smirked as I started moving my mouth up and down.

I'd always been good at slinging back shots, and now, I used my lack of a gag reflex to my advantage. He was a decent size, but I could do this.

I wanted him to want me. The feeling of control was heady. So what if he wasn't looking at me? He was definitely enjoying it. How much could I distract him?

I moved faster, one of my hands encircling the base of his dick as my mouth sucked and licked its way up and down him, saving the most pressure for the top of the head. My other hand came forward to massage his balls, and he just about bucked out of his seat.

Then he set down his controller.

I released him from my mouth. "Keep playing."

He shook his head.

Nice try, but his distraction was half the fun.

"Keep playing, or I won't."

He grabbed the controller instantly and began shooting again.

To reward him, I sucked him deep and hard.

He faltered, his eyes flicking down to me. With one hand, I set a slow rhythm.

His hips jerked a little, but then his eyes were back on the screen. I could hear yelling through the headset. Maybe it was his turn to be criticized.

The thought made me giddy. I leaned forward and deep-throated him.

He sucked in a breath. Mumbling something to his friends online, he pulled off his headset and tossed his controller on the cushion beside him.

I stopped.

His eyes finally met mine, a pleasureful pain reflected in the dilation of his pupils. "You—" he started, but I wasn't done with this game yet. And I kind of didn't want him to talk.

I bent forward. "Shh."

I started stripping. There was no music, no beat. We didn't giggle over how ridiculous it was. There was only him, sitting there, holding his cock outside his shorts on the couch in front of me, his piercing eyes watching as my shirt and pants were peeled off in the low lighting.

Our breathing punctuated the tension in the air as my bra came off, but I didn't give him a ton of time to take in my chest, as my underwear soon followed. I kicked it away.

I stood before him, completely naked. It was a powerful thing, baring myself as he still sat there, almost completely clothed.

He said nothing, his expression wary, waiting.

What would I do next? I didn't even know.

I smiled, and he mirrored me, his mouth quirking up in amusement and arousal.

My hand drifted down to the ache between my legs, and I began to touch myself, my eyes never leaving his as I massaged my clit in slow circles.

He groaned, and his hand snaked out from the couch to catch me, but I evaded him, twisting my hips away as I pressed one finger inside myself. I let out an entirely unnecessary moan for his benefit.

"I want you," he growled.

I wagged my free index finger at him. "My terms."

He sank back into the couch in defeat, but his eyes were still glued to me, the air between us hotter than ever.

I moved my finger, but even though I was already wet, it wasn't the right angle. It wasn't enough. I pulled out, deciding instead to walk toward him.

He grabbed my damp hand when I was a foot away.

My breath caught. *What if …*

I pressed my finger against his lips, and they parted. Without breaking eye contact, he sucked hard, tasting my arousal.

My knees wobbled. I was the one in control here, wasn't I? The line was beginning to blur. Did I want him to give me oral because he put that thought in my head or because I needed it? Ah, fuck it.

But now, how did I ask for it? What did I do?

But he seemed to sense my excitement because when I sat next to him, he gently pushed me down until my head touched the arm of the couch. I spread my legs, resting one on the floor and the other on the top of the couch, completely open to him. He lowered his head, nibbling my stomach, nipping the insides of my thighs. Then without warning, he slipped his thumb inside me.

I groaned. Then before I could even think about what to do, I was threading my fingers through his hair, guiding him to where I wanted. He began sucking on my clit in a delicious, rough sort of way. My back arched off the couch, and he reached up with his other hand and pushed me down. His tongue started to move against me. Though I loved it, the sensation was so intense that I began to shy away from him, scooting my ass farther and farther up the couch.

"I … I—"

But he was having none of it.

He withdrew his thumb and grabbed my hips with his hands, pulling me back down to meet his mouth. His tongue speared into me, his thrusts unrelenting as I climbed higher and higher.

"I'm going to—"

He stopped.

I could have killed him.

In shock, I regarded him, his hands clenching my thighs, my wetness covering his mouth as he stared at me and smiled.

Enough. Wasn't I supposed to be the one in charge? I was going to fuck him and get what I wanted. What I needed.

I jabbed a finger at the package on the side table, and he grabbed the condom and rolled it on, a smirk pulling at the corner of his mouth. Then he obediently sat back up on the couch.

He didn't need further instruction as he grabbed my hips and pulled me on top of him, thrusting into me from below.

We alternated tempos—mine a slower grind that stimulated my clit, his a frenzied fuck that rattled my teeth. When I came, it was fast and hot and dirty. A wet explosion of pleasure.

As the shudders rippling down my spine subsided, the cold of the winter day seemed to seep through the walls and into my entire body. For the first time, I really wanted to cuddle after.

But this guy didn't care. The lights would dim any second. Then he'd throw a, "Confidence," my way and disappear.

For the first time in my short sex life, I started to tear up. *Shit, no. Come on.* God, it was so embarrassing.

Get out. Get out now, I thought frantically, but his warm hands were still on my hips.

There is no reason to cry, damn it! You know what this place is.

I collapsed against his neck, his stupid, floppy hair in my face. He pulled me gently off of him.

When he saw my face, what I was fighting against, his features smoothed, and he wrapped his arms around me, gathering me back into his lap. He still had all his clothes on, save for his dick, and I was naked, exposed. It was supposed to be empowering. It had been.

What's wrong with me?

"Shh," he said, petting my hair. "It's okay."

This wasn't what this room was supposed to be about. I started laughing at the absurdity of it all. It was awkward and frantic, but it was what it was. We sat there a while, his character in the game motionless on the screen while he held me.

When the lights flickered out, he released me.

"It's too bad," he whispered in my ear. "I could've held you all night."

What the …

I sat on the couch as his footsteps faded and the lights clicked back on. He wasn't supposed to say shit like that, was he? That wasn't the line.

I had been over here, trying to separate my love life from my sex life—if that was even possible, if that was even what they were trying to teach me—and he'd broken character.

My skin prickled with goosebumps now that I no longer had the adrenaline of sex and the feel of him against me.

It was a compliment. A compliment and nothing else. You're not looking for a boyfriend or even a fuck buddy with these men, and they don't want that from you either. He's not even your type. He was just a challenge, the way a lot of guys see you. The way Brayan saw you.

Brayan. I hadn't thought about him in a while. But it was there, that betrayal, cropping up at the most inappropriate moment. As I pulled my clothes back on, I desperately tried to erase him from my thoughts and take what the video-game guy had said as something light even though every fiber of me kind of thought that maybe it wasn't. Maybe he'd broken the rules by telling me what he had.

I considered knocking on Tristen's door as I entered the dorm but thought better of it and passed by his room instead. Someone else had just been all over me. I owed it to myself, to Tristen, to this experience to see it through and *then* decide if there was anything between us. Of course, if Bliss told him I was jumping into bed with every dude on campus, there would be a fat chance of that ever happening.

But still, the draw was there, and the next day, instead of going to the library, I slid on my slippers to go study in the common room.

I was the only one there, and it was sort of peaceful to work through the pages of reading and note-taking on my own, a soft soundtrack without lyrics streaming through my earbuds. I hummed as I skimmed through Biology, then Economics. I was just opening my Algebra book when Tristen walked in.

He tried to make it look like he hadn't been looking for me, but I wasn't fooled, and he knew it. Sheepishly, he made his way to my table.

"What's your torture today?"

"Algebra."

I was crap at math. I could erase lots of careers from my path based on this one problem alone. Of course, it would help if I showed up to class instead of sipping booze at a water park.

"Want some help?" He pulled out the chair next to me and straddled it backward.

"You feel like being tortured, too?"

He laughed. "Maybe."

I flipped the book his way, and he ran his finger down the line of numbers, biting his lip. His little frown as he concentrated had me squirming in my seat.

"Okay, here we go." He grabbed my notebook, all business. He scanned what I'd already done and erased the last step. "So, what you need to do is …"

I clicked back into study mode.

An hour later, we were sharing a bag of chips, our heads bobbing along to the same song from my earbuds, while I finished the last problem with a flourish.

"Alright, rock star. There you go." Tristen held his hand up for a cheesy high five.

I smacked it, giggling. "Oh, hey! I got you something. Hang on!"

I dashed back to my dorm room and grabbed the T-shirt I'd seen in the water park gift shop and sprinted back.

I handed it to him, suddenly nervous. "It's a shirt of the game show we watched the other day. It's probably dumb, but it made me think of you."

He laughed, pulling it on over his long-sleeved shirt. "How do I look?"

"Like you're ready to kick some ass."

His megawatt smile dulled. "Hey, can we talk for a minute?"

I knew he didn't mean about math. In the history of forever, there were never three scarier words than *can we talk*.

But we weren't even dating.

Then why did it feel like we were?

I popped out my earbud and sat back down. "Sure."

He handed the other one back to me. "Bliss told me you're kinda going through something right now and I should steer clear." His voice was gentle.

God, why did he have to be gentle?

I said nothing. We looked at each other for a long moment. I had never been good at confrontation, but I couldn't break the serious eye contact.

"Should I?"

"Should you what?" I asked, trying to make sure I answered exactly what he wanted me to.

"Should I steer clear of you?"

It was a complicated question.

I gazed down at the numbers on the page. Math was easier than this, and that was saying something.

"As what?" I fingered the page. *As a friend? A lover? A boyfriend?*

I needed to know where he wanted to go with this. I couldn't lie to myself any longer. I wanted him as more than my friend. It didn't matter that it hadn't been long since Brayan. Tristen was the boy next door with dirty dance moves. He helped me with math and watched stupid shows with me when I was sad. He walked with me, challenged me. Liked me. Every time I tried to push him away, I knew it was morally right, but it felt wrong.

Tension stretched between us as he searched my face, nothing but the heat clicking on to disturb the silence. A lump formed in my throat.

Tell me you want me, so we can date. Tell me you don't, so I don't feel guilty about fucking other guys.

Sometimes, it felt like Brayan wasn't real because what he'd felt for me wasn't real. He didn't get me the way Tristen did. If Tristen and I did date and it ended, I wouldn't be able to sleep with someone else the next day. It would be messy. I was already more attached than was rightfully healthy. If he walked out of my life now, there would be a gap. A hole. And that prospect was frightening as fuck.

"As ..." He ran a hand through his hair, then returned his gaze to mine. "I don't know, Kenzie. We're friends, but we're—"

"I know." I blew a piece of my hair away from my face.

"Right?" He looked taken aback that I was finally being just as direct with him as he was with me.

"I think—"

"I mean, I know that you liked Brayan, and it hasn't been enough time, and I am totally willing to wait until it has. I don't want you to think I'm, like ... I don't know. You're just fun and brave and gorgeous, and you care about school, and I don't know what you're thinking. Like, ever. And I can usually read people, you know? I'm going to shut up now." Red crept up from his collar to cover his cheeks.

His rambling was quite possibly the cutest thing I had ever seen. He thought I was all those things? It made what I was about to say that much harder.

"You should probably steer clear of me this week. But I also don't want you to, and that's not fair. I also know you have no idea what I'm talking about. I have ... a commitment right now." I clasped my hands together on top of the book, wishing I could hold myself together the same way.

"The guy you're seeing at night? The one who made you cry?"

God, he was perceptive. Well, ish. And I didn't want to correct him.

"Not exactly." My eyes flicked away from his.

"Can you tell me what's going on?"

He was so earnest. I wanted to tell him. I was also absolutely horrified. No way in hell could I actually tell this guy what I was doing. Not if I wanted a future with him.

"Um, no," I said slowly. "Not right now anyway," I amended. "Can you give me a couple days? Two days, and I'll be able to make a decision about …" I gestured to the air between us.

"What's going to change in two days, Mackenzie?"

I dropped my head into my hands. I'd be asking the same thing if I were in his position. "I don't know."

Everything. I hoped. This was so confusing.

He was silent for a long moment, then finally nodded once. "Okay," he said, drawing the word out. "Two days it is."

"Two days," I echoed.

He stood, replacing the chair, and then was gone.

After that, I couldn't listen to music, and the pages of equations blurred together. Pressure built in my chest until breathing normally became a joke. I wouldn't remember anything I studied.

I headed back to my dorm and changed my clothes before Modern Lit.

Two days. Two days, and clarity would come—or at least, my experiences in The Hall of Art and Pleasure would end.

I slung my backpack over my shoulder and headed out.

It was unhealthy, I knew, to hinge all my hopes on some kind of revelation in that last room, but that didn't mean I could stop myself from doing it. I'd been through so many things in the house. Mirrors and dark rooms and toys and anal. How much further could the sex even be taken at this point? How much more confident could I get? Would that ruin what Tristen and I could have together?

I had to find out.

16

THE PARTY

There weren't many doors left to choose from in The Hall of Art and Pleasure.

I took my time selecting just the same. Though I'd enjoyed the domination room, I didn't have much desire to be hurt. That left me with only a few doors, each sporting their own painting or sketch. The papers fluttered in a draft that wafted lazily down the long corridor. Though I looked at all of them, giving each a real chance at striking my fancy, this was my last door before the door in the other hallway. The test. This was the last thing I could choose for myself. I wasn't waffling because I was thinking about Tristen.

The painting on the door I finally chose was probably as old as the house itself. How had they gotten the paper to look like that? It read:

"Bacchanalia" by Auguste Levêque, Date Unknown (c. 1900), Belgium

I pulled out my phone and searched for what it meant. What popped up had to do with wild and drunken parties. Well, that made sense. The painting was … interesting. A mix of men and women, all in some way naked, overlapping each other, touching each other, faces slack with a reckless abandon, which was something unfamiliar to the way of life I had known for so long.

I flashed back to my senior year of high school, the conversation I'd had with my über-conservative parents in the spotless living room.

"Absolutely not," my dad lectured from the couch, setting aside his e-reader. "I know what goes on at those parties."

"But it's senior year. The only senior party. Everyone is going." I tried to keep the petulant whine out of my voice.

Telling them had been a mistake. I should have just gone. I calculated the risk of attempting to escape out the basement sliding door and decided against it. They'd be expecting that now. Plus, did that thing even open? We never used it, and I certainly had never snuck out before.

"I sincerely doubt every parent is allowing their kid to go. You'll just be in that percentage of kids who aren't going to wake up tomorrow with permanent marker scrawled across their faces and a hangover to beat all hangovers. Who knows what other things could happen?"

"I won't fall asleep," I argued. "I won't drink anything! I can handle myself. Why don't you trust me? Haven't I earned it?"

"Of course we trust you." My dad rolled his eyes. "We just don't trust other people. And though you're a great kid …" He raked his hand through his short blond hair. "Even great kids do dumb things when they're in big groups."

My mom cut him a glance. "But we do trust you," she tacked on.

"Yeah," I said sarcastically, "sure seems that way."

The tension in the room was high when I heard the answer that followed, the words that ended the conversation once and for all unless I wanted to have consequences for continuing to whine.

"Asked and answered," my dad said.

And that was that.

It wasn't like I hadn't been to a party after I left home. And it wasn't like my parents didn't love me. Even with their strict rules, I knew everything had been done with love. Still, when I'd enrolled in the university, none of the parties felt the way I imagined they would after my father painted that grim picture. I didn't want to wake up in puke with a penis penned on my forehead.

Now, I wondered what it would be like to not care, just for one night. My whole life was so strictly controlled, even now. I was going to find out.

When I opened the door, a wave of noise escaped. Inside, the party was in full swing in what looked like some sort of ballroom. God, these rooms were some kind of soundproof.

Who had commissioned this house? What had they been thinking? Had they already known what it would be used for?

"Heyyy," a chorus greeted me, cheers erupting from both guys and girls.

They had been waiting for me. What if I hadn't shown up? Would they still have partied this way? Was every room going on with their plans? Or did they wait until I chose something to tell everyone else to go home?

I froze. What if I wasn't the only person invited to the hall? What if, after I entered, this room had the paper removed from the door and just looked blank to the next person? What if sexy stuff was happening everywhere around me, in every room?

"You're thinking too hard," a girl said as she bounced up to me.

She bore a striking resemblance to Bliss, down to that mischievous twinkle in her eye. She handed me a red cup of beer, and I downed it.

Tonight, I wasn't going to care about anything. I was finally going to do the college thing—only sexier than I'd ever done it before. I was going to let go.

I started with drinking. My stomach accepted the little green Jell-O shots, a shot of whiskey, and a whole lot of beer from the tables set up around the room. What was the saying? *Beer before liquor, never been sicker*? But I was having liquor before beer, so I must be in the clear. I giggled at the rhyme. Every moment made me more and more loose, my body practically boneless and animalistic, freer than I ever could've imagined.

When no one approached me besides the girl, the alcohol I was drinking made me less lonely. This was a party! I should dance. I sucked down one more Jell-O shot and headed to where a throng of people moved, butts grinding into groins, lips sucking on necks, hands wandering. It didn't seem as shocking as when I had stepped through the door. Maybe it was the alcohol. Maybe it was this place.

By the time I made it to the center of the room, the lights flickered off.

I stumbled, then stayed where I was as black lights lit up one by one on the walls.

"It isn't over," a guy passing by said to me, as if reading my thoughts. "It's just getting started." Then his arms pulled me into the crowd, and the music got louder, the beat becoming heavier, sexier.

There were so many people dancing, no one hanging around on ratty couches or near a keg. We were all one organism, molten and fluid, one being as we danced with each other. Body paint was passed around, and a man with glowing white teeth tore the arms off my shirt and painted me with bold, slow strokes, his eyes never leaving mine. Every place his fingers touched, my skin burned. He could have drawn a dick for all I cared, just like my parents had foretold.

When he passed off the paint to someone else, our eyes locked. We were the only ones in the room not dancing for a split second, and for that same split second, we might've been the only ones in the room at all.

Then he grabbed the front pockets of my skirt and flipped me around until my back touched his chest. His hands splayed against my bare legs and inched up under the short denim.

He sucked in a breath. "You're not wearing any underwear," he whispered in my ear as I laid my head against his shoulder.

"I didn't see the point because I was coming …" I waved my hand at the crowd. The alcohol was definitely affecting me.

"Oh, I'll make you come," he promised.

"Me, too." Another guy appeared in front of me, tall and buff and blond. He began fondling my breasts through the thin fabric of my T-shirt. "You're wearing a lot of clothes." His mouth descended to bite my earlobe.

With their beautiful heads on either side of my face, I was surrounded by sexy males. Two of them. Was this what the room was about? My skin tingled.

"Well—" My head swiveled around drunkenly to see who was watching us. It was dark. Not that dark, though.

One girl swayed in booty shorts and a dark bra as a man stuck his hands into her waistband and grabbed her ass cheeks. Another girl climbed onto a chair, unbuttoning her blouse.

"Hell yeah," a guy cheered from the crowd. He, too, was shirtless, bright swirls of paint circling his nipples.

Was this party getting out of hand? Yes. But it didn't seem dangerous to me. No one was snorting coke in the corner or forcing anyone else to do anything they didn't want to do. We were all having fun.

The blond guy in front of me pulled my arms up, and I giggled as his hands brushed against my rib cage when he slid my shirt over my head.

"Damn," he said when he saw my push-up bra. It was white, and it glowed fluorescent under the black lights.

"I want to paint the rest of your body," the man in front of me said, "but I don't have anything with me. Can I use my tongue?" He stumbled a bit.

What a line! I laughed out loud as he used me to steady himself.

"Oh boy, are you sloppy." The same girl from before approached me. "May I?" she asked, pointing to my bra.

She was entirely naked, and man, did she own it. Her short body, so different from my height, was definitely bottom heavy, and the drunken wannabe "painter" eyed her with no small amount of lust.

"Like you can handle me, big boy," she threw over her shoulder at him.

"A woman always does it better," she said to me, reaching behind me to undo the clasp of my bra.

My mouth hung open in shock as the band around my chest went slack. She pulled the bra from my body, her eyes burning into mine. The way she stared at me was weirdly erotic, even as I leaned back against the guy whose hands were cupping my bare ass now. When her mouth dipped to my breast and her tongue darted out to lick my nipple, I jerked back and almost threw him off-balance.

She laughed throatily and then was immediately distracted. The drunken blond man hugged her from behind. Her legs gave way as he lowered her to the floor.

"Apparently, you can," she gasped, falling to her knees.

"Yes, ma'am." He parted her ass and slammed into her.

Holy fuck.

The warmth from the man behind me—the one with the beautiful, straight, glowing teeth—seeped into my back. His hands, splattered with neon paint, reached around and found my heat, his finger lazily circling my clit as we both watched her get fucked on the floor in time to the beat of the music.

"So hot," he whispered in my ear.

I didn't know if he meant them on the floor, getting it on doggy style, or the temperature of my pussy, or the fact that I was now wet and gasping, wishing it were him doing that exact thing to me. And why shouldn't he?

"Will you—" I asked, then broke off as his finger slipped up inside me.

"Yes?" he asked, chuckling.

"I'm tipsy." I stumbled a little, leaning into him.

"And?"

"And you're not?" It was a question.

"I'm plenty drunk, but not too drunk to fuck you." His mouth fastened to my neck, hungry and hard.

On the floor, the girl cried out as she came, her ass shuddering. Over her, the guy picked up his pace as she collapsed to the ground, fucking her hard until he, too, found release.

When he stood, he pulled his condom off.

"You're next," he said to me.

"But—"

The man behind me was massaging the wall of my vagina now, his finger curling in the most delicious way as he breathed against my neck. God, it was so hot. I tried to fold into myself, my legs shaking, but he followed me, relentless.

"We'll both take you," he growled against my neck.

I swung around, worried suddenly about who could see us. It didn't seem anyone was paying attention, though. In fact, I might be the only person in here still partially clothed. A girl sucked a guy's dick as he lay on the couch. Another guy slammed into a man's ass from behind, a look of painful pleasure on both of their faces.

The blond man tilted my chin up with his hand, one eyebrow arched.

Would I say yes? Could I handle two men at once?

I gulped. "Okay."

The man behind me lowered us to the floor that the other girl had recently vacated. Where had she gone? The room tilted and fuzzed a bit at the edges. It was kind of funny.

He shed his clothes, pulling me on top of him, my skirt inching up until it was more of a belt, my entire ass exposed.

He groaned as I lowered myself inch by inch onto his length.

My hand moved to my breast. I rolled a nipple between my fingers, taking in the fact that there was another couple not far from us, doing almost exactly the same thing. The girl and I shared a glance, then looked away before we both increased our speeds.

"Yes, fuck me." He lay back, his hands behind his head as he watched me bounce up and down.

The blond moved behind me. After a moment, his finger pressed into my ass gently, wet with something already.

I gasped and fell forward, the guy on the floor barely catching me in time.

"Easy," he said to the blond.

"She's so tight," he replied.

"What?" I gasped.

His fingers, in addition to the way the man on the floor moved within me, were making my body tingle.

The tip of a hard dick poked my ass.

"You ever take two guys at once?" the blond's voice asked lowly.

I shook my head, my knees shaking.

"Ah, babe. Let him in," the guy on the ground said, but his voice was muffled because his mouth was full of my breast now.

"Yeah, let me in, so we can both fuck you the way we want to," the blond crooned.

I forced myself to relax my muscles. Little by little, he inched his way in, the sensation so full, so different, that a desperate sound, like a cross between a cry and a question, escaped me.

"We've got you, honey," the guy on the bottom said before catching my mouth in a sweet French kiss.

And then they began the rhythm of fucking me together. In my pussy, out of my ass. In my ass, out of my pussy. Back and forth, back and forth. The pressure in my ass was almost relieved by the pleasure in my vagina, but the shock of it made me come down from where I'd been just moments before, and they could tell.

"Get her around the front," the blond said through gritted teeth. "I want her turned on, and I'm going to come. I—ahh," he cried out against me, his dick pulsing.

The man below me halted as the guy on top pumped into my ass roughly, his hands digging into my butt cheeks.

I whimpered at the loss of the part of the fuck I had been enjoying more, but it was replaced with a hand against my wetness, stroking my clit.

Yes, please.

"I want it. I held off," the guy under me said.

My attention snapped to him. *Was he talking to me or the guy now slipping out of my asshole?* I couldn't tell.

"Fuck, that was hot," a new voice said.

I looked up at a dark, naked, very hard man.

"Suck me a minute," he said as the man under me pushed me off him.

Wait, what? I couldn't keep up with what was going on.

A dick shoved its way past my teeth, and I almost choked, still on my knees.

"Ah yeah, babe. Fuck," he said, his hand at the back of my head as he pushed his way in and out, getting harder each time I gagged.

"Enough," I managed to get out.

He immediately stopped, pulling me to my feet. He lifted me until my legs wrapped around him. Between us, he threw a condom on in record time, and then he was in me.

"Do it," he said, his eyes leaving mine to glance over my shoulder.

The warmth of another body behind me was startling. Yanking my head around, I saw the guy from the floor positioning himself.

He was too big! But I didn't protest as the blunt tip of his dick pressed against me. I only shuddered with apprehension.

"You'll take me. You'll love it," he said. "I'm still wet from your pussy, and now, I want your ass. It's so gorgeous."

They held me still as I nodded against the dark man's clavicle.

The pressure on my hole built, trying to take in the head of him, hurting so good that I could have died. "It's—"

The man behind me grunted. "Jesus, she's so—"

"Get it in," the dark man rumbled. "We need to get her there before we both lose it."

The party was in full swing now, becoming a … what was the word? Orgy? I heard moans through the gaps in the music and could smell the sweet stench of sex in the air. Was everyone in here fucking? I became impossibly wetter.

They might be watching us. The dark man had been.

"She's going to come fast," he said. "Come on."

With a final shove, the man behind me entered me, and they both stilled.

I wanted to scream, but I also needed what I'd been teased with this entire time.

"Fuck," I cried through gritted teeth, my legs still wrapped around the dark man.

They both held my hips and started to fuck me.

In and out, in and out. The rhythm increased, was painful, was pleasurable, was making me get lost in the lights and the dark and the sex in the room. Neither kissed me, both concerned with their dicks in my holes, and I wondered if they could feel each other through the wall inside me. That turned me on even more, and I began climbing toward that peak. My legs started to shake.

"Yes, baby," the man in my ass said. "Let us have you. Come all over us."

When I came, I screamed so hard that the people around us looked on in awe. A flood seemed to gush out of me, startling me as my body contracted and shook.

Holy—what the—

The guys high-fived over my head.

"We made her squirt. Damn, we're good," the guy in my ass said.

They made me what? Is that a thing?

My face colored in shame, but the man behind me—now limp inside me—kissed my neck hard, sucking, as the guy in front of me plundered my mouth with his tongue.

The lights went black, the music stopped, and they let me go, gently setting me back on the floor.

"Confidence," one of them whispered roughly in my ear.

I heard the rustling in the room, and what seemed like seconds later, I was standing in full light, my body dripping in the aftermath of the best party I'd ever been to.

Red Solo cups, Jell-O shots, condoms, and God knew what else littered the floor.

I still shook, my hand fluttering to my neck. Had I just gotten my first hickey? It didn't bother me.

Numbly, I readjusted my skirt and found my shirt, pulling it back over my chest with wooden movements. As I padded back down the hall and out the door of the house on Maple, my body became heavier, battling against the cold wind on the way home with steps that weren't half as fast as they normally were.

Was I tired? Was it the alcohol? Or something else entirely?

17

TAKE THE SIX

Bliss and I walked to breakfast together the next morning in silence. We grabbed egg white omelets as I tried to formulate what to say. Bliss's rage always came out in the quiet, and it was so uncomfortable I wanted to scream. At the same time, I couldn't be mad at her for getting whiplash. She had no idea what was going on.

We slid into seats at the end of a long table, and I took a sip of orange juice for courage.

"Alright, that's it. I don't even know why we're fighting!"

I hid my smile. She always beat me to it.

"Me neither." *Liar.*

"So, let's be done. I need my friend back, so I can tell you about Tony." She grabbed my arm and gave me puppy-dog eyes. They weren't necessary.

"Tell me about Tony."

Her smile lit up the whole room. "Thank God. Okay, so he's totally gorgeous, right?"

"Right." If you liked super-tall, beefy guys.

"He hasn't asked me out yet. Can you believe that?"

I tilted my head. "The horror."

"I'm serious! I mean, we made out twice, so I know he's into me, but I want to be more than that, and I'm dying."

I speared a bite of omelet with my fork. "So, ask him out."

"Okay, so don't get mad."

I narrowed my eyes and took a bite of sausage.

"I did kinda ask him on a date, but it became a group thing. So, you and Tristen are coming, too."

So this was why she was breaking her silence. "Didn't you tell Tristen to steer clear of me?"

"Shit. Yes. Are you mad?"

I raised my eyebrows.

"I'm sorry! He was adorable, and my mouth had a mind of its own. You know I can't control myself sometimes."

"Understatement of the year," I muttered.

"I know you're sleeping with someone else, but it wouldn't have to be a double date, I swear. Just keep him company while I figure out Tony."

"Where are we going?" If it was a dark movie theater, I was out.

"Mini-golfing."

That … might work. Even if it didn't, I still owed her for the trash friend I'd been lately.

"I don't know," I teased. "Mini-golfing is kind of lame."

"You need to hang out with me," she begged. "And you can't deny you had a great time the last time we hung out with them."

Yeah, that was the problem. I couldn't feel that way about someone until I was done with Maple House. It wouldn't be fair.

"The way you danced, Kenz. Seriously, I've never seen you cut loose like that."

I pushed my messy hair back, securing it in a half-bun with the ever-present hairband I kept around my wrist. I'd been cutting loose a lot lately. Just not in any way I could tell Bliss.

"How do you do that and still look good?" she whined. "I want curly hair."

I rolled my eyes. No, she didn't.

She turned her big, sad eyes to where the boys were sitting two tables down. They were surrounded by people, but Tristen had on a pair of glasses this morning, his bloodshot eyes betraying some kind of debauchery last night. They just made him hotter. Like a blond Clark Kent.

Some girl was hanging on to his every word as he picked at his eggs. God, she was so obvious.

But Bliss wasn't looking at Tristen. She was gazing at Tony, her expression slack-jawed and totally entranced.

"I guess we could go mini-golfing," I conceded. "If it's in that new indoor one."

"Like we'd be able to do it outside in this weather," she mocked. "Wait, are you saying yes?" She squealed, bouncing around in her seat.

The boys' attention shifted to us through the crowd.

"She said yes!" Bliss yelled to them.

Embarrassed, I covered my face with my hands, bracing my elbows on the table. When I dared to peek out again, Tristen was laughing. He raised his glass of water toward me with a promise in his eyes. Of fun and something else I couldn't quite place, but it made a sickly-sweet weight settle in the pit of my stomach. We held each other's stare for a few beats too long before the girl sitting next to him stood and marched off.

The spell was broken as we both watched her leave. Tristen frowned in puzzlement, and I felt a sick satisfaction I didn't want to analyze too much.

Good riddance.

Tristen groaned as his ball bounced off the clapboard for about the millionth time, and I hid a giggle.

"You, Miss Golf Specialist," he said, pointing his club at my chest, "you're such bad luck. I've never sucked at mini-golf until today. It has to be you."

He lined up another shot and finally got his orange ball through the little house. It was his fifth shot, and he still wasn't positioned right to make it in the hole.

I sighed loudly. "Just take the six, Tristen."

"No way." He lined up his shot again. This time, he hit the ball much too hard.

I pressed my lips together, laughter bubbling painfully inside me.

"Don't even say it," he threatened, his voice exasperated.

"Take the six," I singsonged.

"Ugh, fine."

He picked up his ball, leaving me with the perfect sight of his backside. Damn, he had a great ass.

Bliss and Tony were about three holes ahead of us because of Tristen's stubbornness and Tony's desire to be alone with Bliss. It was just as well. They'd be a cute couple, and Tony had proven himself trustworthy in the club.

The club. My skin tingled as Tristen and I walked, our bodies too close as we approached the next hole. What was it about nightclubs that made people forget their personal boundaries in such slutty ways? And now, I was supposed to act normal every time I remembered Tristen's warm body against mine, the hard muscles of his arms flexing as they'd held me.

I snuck a glance at him, but he was the picture of nonchalance. Maybe it was just me who struggled with that.

"Want to play a game?" His voice was low and startling.

I cleared my throat. "I thought we were."

"Kenzie, you're killing me. Let's play a better one."

"Okay," I said. "But for the record, I'm enjoying kicking your ass at this."

"I bet." He grinned. "How about I ask a question and you answer, and then we switch?"

"Okay," I said uncertainly.

It wasn't really a game. He was trying to get to know me. It was the kind of thing you did with a girl you wanted to date. We'd drawn the line clearly before that stage, put everything on pause until my two days were up. Right?

Except I could still feel his hands on my thighs, my ass cradled by his hips, the bass from the speakers thrumming through us as we dirty danced.

Yeah, that line is super strong.

"Okay, I'll start," he said. "What's your family like?"

"It's just me and my parents. They're still together, sending me care packages so I don't starve. What about you?"

"Just my mom and me. Dad died when I was two."

I looked up, but he made a show of seeing where Bliss and Tony were.

"I'm sorry."

"Nah, it's kind of like … she said she'd never find another guy like him. Never remarried. They had this be-all, end-all romance. I grew up believing in that," he said.

I smiled as I lined up my next shot. It explained him.

"What's your major?" I asked as I tapped the ball with my putter.

"Uh, I'm finishing up my gen ed courses and getting into more math stuff." He frowned when my ball fell into the hole. "I'm working on the engineering thing."

Engineering? He should be a counselor.

"Yeah, I thought about it. I want to be able to take care of my mom financially, though."

Crap. Did I say that out loud?

"I'm sorry," I said. "It's none of my business. No wonder you were able to help me with my math yesterday."

He raised an eyebrow, then hit the ball without lining it up. A new strategy. The ball rolled until it was two inches from the hole. He smiled that megawatt smile.

"I'm still going to win," I taunted him.

He waited until I was completely lined up with the shot on the next hole before asking his question. Then when I swung my club back, he asked, "When did you lose your virginity?"

My shot went wide, bouncing off the obstacle rocks and ending up in a hard-to-putt-from corner.

"You did that on purpose," I accused, pointing my club at his chest.

He smirked. "You don't have to answer."

"Eighteen." I never backed down from a challenge.

He let me wedge my club between my ball and the wall, and I sank my putt in silence. Great. It was the wrong answer. Maybe he was being polite and letting it go. It was my turn to ask after all.

I opened my mouth to ask his favorite color when he asked, "High school eighteen or college eighteen?"

"Does it matter?" Eighteen was eighteen.

"Yeah, kinda. High school eighteen is like *long-term boyfriend* kind of sex. College eighteen is … well, it could be anything."

He was trying to read me. He probably had a theory, like the one about where people sat during a lecture.

"College eighteen."

He cocked his head to the side. "Surprising."

I leaned on my club and met his eyes. "Why?"

"You're kidding," he scoffed.

"Nope."

"Come on, Kenzie. You know what you look like. I'm surprised no one talked you into it earlier."

I ducked my head, chafing at such an over-the-top compliment. "Stop that."

"You had to have heard that before." His voice was incredulous as he sank the putt.

I hadn't actually, but he didn't need to know that.

I changed the subject back to safe territory. "It's my turn."

We continued in that way, asking and answering questions, some personal, though not quite as personal as that one. I didn't have the courage to ask him when he had lost his virginity. What would the answer prove to me anyway?

By the time we finished the course, Bliss and Tony were waiting for us. Well, kind of. They were making out on the bench near the exit.

Tristen's eyes met mine, and we shared a moment of mirth. Then he cleared his throat, but they didn't separate.

"Bliss."

She wanted more than a make-out with Tony. It would be better to leave him wanting more.

She waved me away.

"Bliss, if you don't stop it, I'm going to tell Tony about the time that you got that fraternity guy to—"

She unlocked her lips from his in a hurry. "We should go," she said breathlessly to him.

"What fraternity guy?" he asked, looking from her to me.

"Nothing," she said, shooting me a death glare.

I laughed.

"Mackenzie is obviously crazy," she assured him.

"Obviously." He narrowed his eyes, and then they were up and following us to the car.

When we got back to the dorm parking lot, I hung around Tristen's door for a minute as Tony and Bliss walked ahead.

"This was ..." What? It wasn't a date. Why was I acting like it was? I told myself I was giving Bliss some space to say good-bye to Tony.

Behind Tristen, an old analog clock on the wall clicked ominously.

Shit, the test! At this rate, I'd barely make it to Maple House on time. Mini-golf and Tristen had been so absorbing that I hadn't even properly freaked out about what would be behind door number eight.

"I have to go, but ..."

He swept a curl behind my ear with his fingers. Then he kissed my cheek. "Yeah, me, too," he said.

That small patch of skin burned all the way back to my dorm room. Though it wasn't anywhere near the crazy, sordid things I'd been doing lately, a weight settled low in my stomach that had nothing to do with sex and everything to do with the way I was beginning to feel about Tristen.

Maybe that was why, when I entered the now-familiar door of Maple House that night, my palms were sweating despite the frigid temperature outside and I was breathing hard. The walk over here had provided me with lots of time to freak out over passing whatever sexual test was inside and whether I should be participating at all when what I really wanted to do was cuddle up with Tristen and let him make me feel special.

After the party, I had a hard time imagining what could possibly take that experience to another level, a higher level, without making me incredibly uncomfortable. To be honest, if I hadn't been a little tipsy, I wouldn't have been able to do what I did—let a girl strip me, let two guys have me, and then … and then some more. But I hadn't been drunk. I couldn't blame the alcohol. My face flushed crimson.

How much I'd learned in the past week, how vast the world of sex seemed to me now even though I knew there were still unexplored kinks out there. And I'd learned—I *thought* I'd learned what they wanted me to. That sex and love weren't the same thing. If I wanted to, I could go out now and do it without getting super attached. I knew that love was separate even if that wasn't how I'd been raised or how I wanted to feel sometimes at the end of the day. It was time to end this.

When I pulled open the heavy wooden door, all was the same as it always was, but when I reached the intersection of hallways, my feet turned and walked in the direction of the hallway I'd never been down.

To the test.

What kind of test? If I didn't want it, could I leave? Of course I could. That was what the contract had said, hadn't it? That I could walk out? I was surprised to find that I hadn't thought about that in a while. I hadn't seriously considered it when I was being challenged inside the rooms. It was a talent of this house—to completely immerse a person in the fantasies it created. The fantasies it fulfilled.

My feet carried me to the solitary door in the long hallway, and though I hadn't expected it, this one had a piece of paper attached to it, too. Another poem, though this time, it seemed weird to read it, knowing I had no other choice but to enter or leave.

XXXI

Because I liked you better
Than suits a man to say,
It irked you, and I promised
To throw the thought away.

To put the world between us
We parted, stiff and dry;
'Good-bye,' said you, 'forget me.'
'I will, no fear,' said I.

—A. E. Housman

I blinked, trying to process the words. *The world between us. Good-bye.* It was appropriate for the last door, to be sure. But wasn't it hitting the nail right on the head? Wasn't it a little … obvious?

I twisted the doorknob, the click of its release echoing down the hallway. My heart thumped wildly as I inched it open, but when my cowardly self finally entered through the door, it was only to find a normal bedroom. In fact, it looked exactly like my dorm room.

I walked forward to touch the bedspread, just one shade darker than the blue of my own. My personal knickknacks were missing, but everything else … it was almost too close for comfort. Or maybe it was for comfort. I didn't know. I pulled my coat off and put it on the hook I was so familiar with. Then I pulled my hair out of its bun, and my boots came next. I pushed them near the door, as I did in the dorm I shared with Bliss.

When I turned back around, I stopped dead. From the wrinkled shirt down to the faded jeans, the guy standing in the doorway was more than familiar.

"Hey, Mackenzie."

Brayan.

18

THE TEST

Frozen, my eyes traveled over him again. I couldn't help myself. Brayan's familiar stubble, the slight wave in his hair. His beautiful skin, so much browner than my own. I'd noticed that when we made love—the contrast of his body against mine.

No.

Not made love.

Had sex.

Brayan didn't love me.

I folded my arms over my chest, though we were both still fully clothed.

"What are you doing here?" My voice was calm, but my words were sharp.

A week ago, I wouldn't have been able to meet his eyes. Now, I stared him down, wanting him to see the anger and hurt he'd caused me.

"I'm your test."

He shoved his hands in his pockets and rocked back, the dimple showing in his left cheek as he smiled. It was a thing I'd thought was so cute, so innocent when we met. A guy with a dimple couldn't possibly be a bad person, right?

He was my test.

"What exactly are you supposed to test?" I asked. "How much I've learned about having sex?"

He chuckled. "Nah, you were always a quick study. Haven't you figured out the point of this week, the name of the game you're playing now?"

I leveled one concise nod at him.

Confidence. It was just a hairsbreadth away from emotional detachment. Maybe that was the real lesson.

"So then, there's only one question." His hand ran over a book on the desk next to him. A prop in a room meant to bring up the memory of our stolen moment together.

"No. There are many."

His eyebrows rose. "There's only one that matters."

But I shook my head. "I'm not playing that way. You have to answer something for me first."

"Always so difficult," he muttered.

"Were you ever actually interested in me?"

He sighed. "Mackenzie ..." His eyes skittered to the side, avoidant and obvious.

"Answer the fucking question, Brayan." I needed to hear him say it even though I already knew the answer from his reaction.

He stared at me; no doubt surprised at my language. But what reason did I have to be polite at this point? He didn't deserve polite. He didn't deserve the Mackenzie he'd seen while I thought we were dating.

Unbidden, thoughts of Tristen entered my head. I never acted around him. I was just … me. I shook away the thought as Brayan answered.

"I wanted you. Sexually. I thought you got that. I thought you were doing what a lot of girls do. You know, stretching the whole thing out, so you didn't feel like …" He shrugged, still not meeting my eyes.

"Like what?" I squared my shoulders. "Like a slut? Having sex doesn't make you a slut."

He nodded. "You *are* learning."

It was so condescending. *What a douchebag.*

"Fuck off," I said and started for the door.

"So, you won't answer the question."

I paused. "You didn't ask one."

"You didn't let me."

"For God's sake, Brayan." I turned to face him.

"Are you still attracted to me? Do you still want me, Mackenzie? Not my personality. My body."

I strode toward him. When I was inches away, I went in for a kiss.

His eyes narrowed in excitement.

When he was less than an inch from my face, I reared back and slapped him hard.

He held his cheek in his hand, eyes burning with resentment. "I didn't think you had it in you," he spat.

"Well, you don't really know me, do you?" I returned.

"So, leave," he suggested.

I should, but …

"I have another question."

He arched a perfect eyebrow. God, what did the guy do, pluck them to be that flawless?

"Did you sign me up for this …" I waved my hand at the room. "Was this you? Did you set this up?"

"Would you believe me if I told you no?"

I searched his face, but I couldn't tell if he was lying or not.

"You don't care anyway." He smiled.

God, I hated that smile.

"I should." I should care a lot whether Brayan was behind this. It would be mortifying. Harassment at best, totally weird and illegal at worst.

"You don't care for the same reason I don't. You want hate sex."

"What?"

"Hate sex. You want it, with me. Use me, Mack. Use me for my body the way I used you."

He leaned in to kiss me, but I pressed my hand to his chest.

"No, thanks."

Why was I being so polite? He didn't deserve that. And why couldn't I breathe right? It had to be the stupid tears I was blinking back. It was always harder to breathe when I cried.

"Come on," he said, pushing against my hand.

"No."

This was different. I didn't know what was happening here, what test I was failing right now, but I couldn't believe that emotional detachment was the point of this whole experience. Could I shut my brain off and fuck him until I got the orgasm he owed me? Was I still physically attracted to him? I was ashamed that the answer to both questions was yes. It was tempting to be the taker for once with him. It would satisfy my sense of justice as much as it would my body.

But … he had been a liar when we dated, and I didn't believe anything he said now. I didn't have to do this. The thought of him getting any pleasure from me made me want to hurl all over his shirt. I didn't want to have sex with him, and I wouldn't do it to pass some stupid test.

I straightened my shoulders. "Stop." The one word that would end the experience for good. The one in the contract. Screw Maple House, The Hall of Art and Pleasure, whatever this was.

Brayan stepped back, his face twisting in shock.

"Fuck you," I whispered, stepping back.

I gathered my coat and slipped my boots back on at the door.

He sighed behind me as I reached for the doorknob. "You passed, you know."

I paused. "I know."

But the lights didn't dim. The one time I needed them to.

What else was there?

I walked out without looking back.

Snow swirled around me as I made my way back to my dorm. Adrenaline made my steps quick, but soon, it faded, leaving me feeling accomplished and empty at the same time. The door to Maple House would never open to me again. It didn't need to. It had done its job.

Confidence? I'd mastered that. I'd won.

As I trekked down the long hallway of identical doors in the dorm, I thought about next year. When I had an apartment, whether it was with Bliss or on my own, I'd have a lot more privacy to have sex. But the prospect of that didn't excite me much. And I was out of breath again, burned out from this week.

Tristen removed his headphones when I trudged by his open door, and I waved emptily at him but didn't pause.

Still, he managed to catch up to me in the hallway in a matter of seconds.

"You okay?" he asked, his hands stuffed in his pockets. "You look upset."

"It's been a weird week," I wheezed.

He frowned. "Have you been running?"

"Something like that." Running away from him. And now Brayan. There had been a lot of running.

"Alright?"

"Yeah." I didn't elaborate.

I couldn't talk about it. Even if I could, I didn't want to.

I unlocked my dorm room and paused with my hand on the knob. "Don't hate me for not asking you in right now," I said to the door.

"Can I check on you tomorrow?"

"Sure," I said, my eyes unseeing.

Inside the dorm, I shed my clothes and took a shower. I hated that I'd even touched Brayan. Scrubbing myself until my skin was shiny pink, I tried to wash away everything that had happened tonight. But I couldn't. All I could console myself with was the fact that I'd done the right thing. When it was time, I'd walked away.

My breathing finally slowed, though the hitch in my chest refused to go away. I put on my comfiest sweatpants and hoodie and crawled into bed with wet hair.

The week was over, and I'd never be so naive again. A relief and a curse.

The next morning, I made my way to the dining commons alone. Bliss was still asleep, having gone to some sports bar with Tony the night before. Her gentle snores had almost been adorable as I snuck out, wearing the sweats I had slept in. I had been up most of the night, thinking, and now, I was starving. I didn't want the crappy food in our room. At least in the dining commons, it was hot crappy food.

I stood in line at the omelet station, only a few other students up at the beginning of the food hours.

When I sat down by myself, I wasn't lonely. I didn't mess around with my phone or read a book. I enjoyed each bite of my food even though it didn't taste like much, relishing in the fact that I could space out. I didn't have to think at all.

The way back to my room to get dressed was like walking through peanut butter. I couldn't shake my mental fog. When I finally reached our door, I pressed my forehead against it.

The lack of sleep is catching up to me, I told myself. *That's all it is.*

I could hear the sound of Bliss talking inside the room and the low reply that no doubt belonged to Tony. Maybe they were going out now. Maybe they were having sex. Either way, I couldn't go in.

Pressing my back against the cool of the concrete wall next to the door, I felt my legs collapse under me as I slid to the floor.

I sat there a long time, holding my key, staring at the white wall across from me. The concrete was much the same as it had been in high school. Painted blocks stacked on top of each other in an alternating pattern. My eyes traced the pattern as time drew a blank. Like I was put on pause or something.

After a while, I zeroed in on a voice. Not a roommate. Not a girl even. But a guy. Tristen.

He waved his hand in front of my face, and I wanted to say something. Something like, *Go away*, or, *I'm okay*, or even, *Please help me.*

But I'd been frozen too long. And then he was gone.

That was fine. Let me live in this suspended animation. Maybe it was good for me. Maybe I didn't care if it wasn't.

Until I heard the scratch of someone sliding down the wall next to me. Until the cold of a Diet Coke can was pressed into my limp hand. But no words were said. None to decipher anyway. With astronomical effort, I turned my head. Tristen again. Sandy hair. Intense eyes. And a Diet Coke. He stared at the wall across from me, too, so I went back to doing that. But his warmth seeped through his long-sleeved shirt and into my body, slowly waking me up, until moments later, I was able to pop the tab on my drink and lift it to my lips.

"Thank you," I said. I didn't even have the energy to be embarrassed that I looked like shit in front of him in my oversize sweats and messy bun.

He nodded at the wall.

I didn't know how long we remained there—me taking fragile little sips of Diet Coke, him not saying anything, not reaching for me, not reminding me that my two days were up. It didn't seem like he was waiting for my answer, but I knew that, eventually, I would have to give him one.

"Want to go to my room?" he asked.

I stood and floated along behind him, a little rain cloud to his sunshine.

We watched his silly game show on his futon again, but this time, he pulled me against him, and I let him.

After the first episode, his eyes met mine, and I dropped my wall for once. Let him see the vulnerability there. Let him see how conflicted I was.

"Yes?" he said, and I knew the real question he was asking.

"Yes," I whispered.

Then his lips were on mine, so gentle, almost reverent. It was too much. But, oh, how I wanted it in this moment. How I wanted to be taken care of, not exploited.

His hands were feather soft on my stomach as he pushed them, inch by inch, under my sweatshirt. Our kisses deepened, and we sank into the futon, him shifting above me until he settled over me, cradling my face with one hand while his other explored.

"So sweet," he murmured.

I broke away. I wasn't sweet. Not anymore. "I—"

"I don't want to push you." He adjusted his shirt, and we both sat back up, folding into our own spaces the way strangers did, careful not to touch each other.

It all came back to sex.

Then his eyes drifted to my neck before I could fix the way my oversized sweatshirt had slouched over one shoulder. Before I realized what he must be seeing. The hickey.

"Tristen, it's not—"

"It's not what? It's not like you're sleeping with everyone but me? I don't want that from you. I mean, I do, but—"

"I know!" I cried. "I didn't want to ruin this. It's just that I was in the middle of something. Something that—" I broke off, fear keeping me from finishing the sentence.

But it was too late. Recognition rocked his features.

"You're *that* Mackenzie?" he whispered, sitting against the back of the futon. "I should have known. Ten o'clock, right? God, I'm so stupid."

"Wha—how could you possibly know that?"

19

YOU MAKE ME SICK

This can't be happening.

There was no way he could know what went on at Maple House. My mind raced as I tried to comprehend that Tristen—beautiful, innocent, earnest Tristen—of all people, had the inside scoop on what had been happening to me this week.

It was like a bomb had gone off in the room.

"You had sex with different guys for a week," he said woodenly, staring straight ahead.

I couldn't process. I sniffled. "Tristen, I'm so—"

"Wrecked? That's what it does to you. Did you learn the lesson, Kenzie? Are you *confident*? Able to do it without feeling a thing?"

I sat back.

"Well?" he demanded.

Don't do this, I wanted to tell him. *Don't go to that place. Don't look at me that way.*

"You don't get to judge me. I asked you to wait. I wasn't going to …" I swallowed. "I wasn't going to start anything while I was still …"

"So, instead, you learned how to shut down. I'm sorry. That's not what I want. I can't—"

"Because I slept with other men?"

"No," he said roughly. "Because you learned what they wanted you to." He pressed his fingers into his eyes.

Now, he was doing that thing people did when they were trying not to cry? I'd done this to him. To us. Anxiety and regret twisted my gut. He had to understand. I had to make him get it. I'd *passed*. I'd said *no*.

But I was too angry with him to care if he got it.

"And what? I'm supposed to be like I was before? Letting men use me, falling for all the wrong ones?"

His face was red when he tried to meet my eyes. "If you don't put yourself out there, you'll never find anyone. Be with anyone. Be as vulnerable as you need to be in order to actually—I can't do this. Not with you," he said.

What the hell was that supposed to mean?

"Please," he choked out, pointing to the door.

I stood and stalked out of the room.

Only once I closed his door did I cry the way I needed to. Great, big, choking sobs.

I was so confused. I was so fucked.

I ran down the hall, wishing for once that we didn't live so close. As soon as I pulled open the door, Bliss stood. Tony must've left.

"What the hell is going on?" She hugged me tight to her chest, and I let her.

I tried to tell her through sobs. "Tristen—"

She let go of me and started for his room.

"Don't!" I pleaded. "Bliss!"

He was as screwed up as I was.

But she had already padded over to his closed door. "Tristen, you bastard!" she yelled as she pounded on his door. "You asshole! You don't deserve her!"

Oh God. She was making everything worse. I stumbled into my room and collapsed on my bed. I couldn't even breathe. I was so embarrassed.

Minutes later, Bliss's hand patted my back. "Calm down," she said, handing me a bottle of water.

I sat up, and she looked at me expectantly.

I needed to tell her.

Just as soon as I caught my breath.

When I was finally able to do more than look pathetic, the whole story came tumbling out. All the sexy things, all the rooms I had been in, all the things I was going through with Tristen, the ups and downs, everything. As I choked out the saga of my sexual transformation, she did what she did best—react. She was a captive audience, gasping and swearing in all the right places. My throat hurt so much from crying and talking that by the time I was done, I was exhausted. I couldn't even cry anymore.

"Holy fuck," she said. "We should go there."

"No. It will be locked now. I told you."

"There's a hooker house just outside campus, and we can't go there?"

"It's not a hooker house. It's …" *Totally a hooker house.* "I don't know if they're getting paid."

Because if they weren't, it was just a sex house. I would feel better if it were only a sex house. That the men had wanted me. Wanted the fantasy. All of it was so mysterious.

But Bliss wasn't satisfied. "Then we'll ask Tristen. From what you've told me, he seems to know about it."

"I can't do that," I whispered, my voice hoarse.

"Oh, you don't have to. I'm going to," she said, bracing her hands on her knees as she got to her feet. "Enough's enough. I'm tired of watching you struggle. Watching you go through shit you shouldn't have to, trying to figure it out all on your own. Tristen needs to pay up, and he's going to do it in information."

"No. Please. Just give me tonight. Let me be sad without bringing any more drama into it. I just need …"

"You need a hug."

I nodded like the pathetic wimp I was. Then I let her cuddle me in bed as the tears I couldn't control ran in rivers down my cheeks until, finally, I succumbed to sleep.

The next morning, I did something I rarely did. I sat down at Bliss's vanity and had her do my makeup. Her concerned expression as she brushed and contoured my face was something I didn't know how to change, even as she tried to chatter away the silence. But I could give her this. I could let her cover the puffy eyes that didn't know how to stop crying. I could let her paint over my swollen face.

Then I let her choose my clothes—leggings and a loose tunic dress over a push-up bra that made me look like I had more going on than I did.

It was finally thawing outside, which meant we were all going without coats even though we technically shouldn't be. It didn't matter. The cold was bone deep. It wasn't the kind of thing layers of clothing could fix.

I got a few looks, but I couldn't tell if it was because of my newly fixed face or if it was because of how depressed I was, apparent even through all the makeup. I forced myself not to frown. Not to do anything. Blank was the best I could do.

I sighed as I walked through the doors to the Economics lecture hall. How had this become the most dreaded class of all time? In the front, Brayan flexed his muscles for a trio of giggling girls. In the back, Tristen snuck in late. His presence radiated toward me.

I was stuck in the middle. Hadn't that always been the case? And now, my purgatory, my hell, was that I was trapped in the center of my own destructive behavior. I had known The Hall of Art and Pleasure was too good to be true.

I avoided Tristen's eyes on the way out. His eyes that saw everything, that saw me.

But he followed.

"Kenzie," he said, his voice quiet as we walked together toward the dorm. "You look different."

"Okay," I said, trying to keep my voice even.

I didn't want to feel anything because, unlike class, there was no middle ground here. I wanted him. He didn't want me. We couldn't unknow the things we did.

When we reached the courtyard outside the dorm, he stopped. I stopped with him.

"You're dressed differently. You did your face."

I shook my head at the crack on the sidewalk. "Bliss did my face."

"It's not you," he said simply.

I laughed bitterly. "You don't like me anyway."

He took a step toward me. "Look ... I was shocked. I should have seen it, but I didn't. I tried to come by this morning, but you were gone. I know I was an ass, but with my experience, well … I didn't react well."

No. He sure as fuck hadn't.

"And what is your experience?"

He opened his mouth like he was going to tell me, but then he closed it, a look of anguish on his face. Then he turned and left me there in the cold.

I didn't know how long I stood there, but after a few moments, my brain suddenly clicked, and everything became clear. Tristen knew about The Hall of Art and Pleasure. Everything inside it. Either he'd been a Maple House case or … *no.*

No, no, no, no, no.

I entered the dorm and took the stairs instead of the elevator. I might be exhausted and out of breath at the top, but I'd be damned if I ran into him again before I knew the truth.

When I got to my dorm, I counted down the hours and minutes, measured in episodes of mindless sitcoms and forced study sprints, all the while thinking, *No. Not Tristen. He couldn't be.*

The clock ticked over to nine forty-five, and I got my coat.

Ten minutes later, I stood in front of Maple House. It wouldn't be open to me. I knew that. Still, I had to try. I had to know.

I climbed the stairs and twisted the knob, holding my breath. Locked.

Well, that was that. I turned to go, but a draft of warmth followed me.

A window was cracked near a table of candles in the corner, probably to let the smoke out.

Before I knew what I was doing, I scrambled onto the windowsill, pulled the window open the rest of the way, and climbed through, being careful to put out the candles with wet fingertips. I didn't want to set the place on fire.

Even though my muscles all tensed as I waited to be reprimanded, to be thrown out, nothing happened. I wasn't stupid enough to think I hadn't made any noise. A chill ran up my spine. I turned and closed the window behind me.

Then I walked down The Hall of Art and Pleasure. There weren't many rooms I hadn't chosen, so I'd start at the beginning. At the door I'd skipped.

I stood outside the room that promised oral and twisted the knob.

A blond man stood in the center of the room with his back to me. The toned back that tapered down into black jeans was one I'd never seen without a shirt before, but it didn't matter.

"Hello, Hannah," he said.

When he turned around, I was already shaking my head.

Tristen.

He closed his eyes, his face pinching in distress. Then he opened them again. "What are you doing here, Kenzie? Your week is up."

I lost it. "You fucking hypocrite! You made me feel like such a slut for doing this when you've been a mystery Maple House man the entire time!" My chest hitched painfully as I wrung my hands. I really wanted to wring his neck instead.

He expelled a gust of air and stepped forward.

I scooted back a step.

He paused, assessing me.

My head swiveled wildly to take in the room. The dim lights. The double-wide couch with no arms in the corner. Plush carpet everywhere. The oral room.

My Tristen, my innocent puppy-dog dorm neighbor, was a part of this, which meant his entire personality around me had been a lie. Just like he was lying to me now.

His tone was gentle but firm when he took another step forward. "I didn't mean that you were a slut at all. I tried to explain. It's not about the sex. It's—"

"It's about the thing you're trying to *teach* through sex. The thing *you* are a part of! How many women have you been *teaching* the same lesson to, Tristen? And what if—God, what if I'd selected this door?"

My eyes widened. Would he have switched dorms? Would he have even been allowed to speak to me, or would it have been like when I tried to talk to the guy from the mirrored room on campus?

"But you didn't choose this door." His arms were open wide, cajoling.

Everything was cut and dry to him. Maybe he really did compartmentalize all of this. Here, he could be a sex god, and at the dorm, he could be a completely different person. How did that even work?

"I wish I had. I wish I had known this about you from the start. I never would have considered—"

"Now, who's the hypocrite?"

And he was right. What was so bad about being experienced? But I already missed him, missed my Tristen, the one who had been happy just to be near me. Now, I knew it was because he had been getting off with who knew how many women at the same time, and I had been doing the same thing with men. We were even, and it should have fixed it, but it didn't. It broke everything even more.

"I don't even know you," I whispered, my voice scratchy.

I coughed once, and his expression turned concerned.

"Are you getting sick?"

"Don't—don't do that."

I couldn't let him be the guy I wanted right now. He couldn't be both men.

He pulled away and gestured to his half-naked body. "I haven't changed. I am who I've always been."

"And who are you, Tristen? Are you the guy who teaches me not to care or the one who judges me for being that way?"

And laid out exactly like that, exactly the way it was, made Tristen's face go pale. Maybe he hadn't truly gotten it until this moment, but I certainly did.

By now, I was sobbing, snot running down my face. I hugged my coat close to me. I had known this was what I'd find when I came here tonight, but I'd hoped I wouldn't. I should never have come back here.

"I hate you," I whispered.

Tristen recoiled as if he'd been slapped. "You—"

He started for me, but I was already out the door.

He didn't follow. Heaven forbid he skip *fucking Hannah* tonight to come after me.

Anger made me forget the walk home, but when I entered the dorm room, I couldn't get warm. It was probably my body going into shock from recent events.

I stood under the spray of the shower, letting the water hit my back and hair. It still didn't help. I tried to breathe, but all I could manage were shallow little sips of air.

I hid under my blankets and some of Bliss's, too. Maybe if they were heavy enough, they could force me back to reality—or at least to sleep.

I was in The Hall of Art and Pleasure, only this time, the walls were a little shaky. I opened the last door, the door with the whip and the suspension rig. It was Tristen. Tristen in leather pants.

He grabbed my wrists. "I want to play a game," he said.

189

"No, not my Tristen," I moaned.

We were on the set of a game show, and Tristen was my coach. I just had to get past the wall ramp, and we'd be fine.

"You're going to be great," he said, kissing me on the cheek. "I could never be as strong as you."

Images blended into one another.

Tristen walking me home from a lecture. Tristen, his face slack with alcohol, basking in the pleasure of dirty dancing with me. Tristen smirking as I concentrated during the great nacho challenge. Tristen, his blond head diving between the legs of a girl who wasn't me.

"No …"

I was so cold. So cold. Why was it so damn cold, and why was I sweating?

Tristen's face was above me. "How long has she been this way?"

"Like, a day and a half. I can't carry her to the doctor by myself. Believe me, I wish Tony were home instead." Bliss's voice was thin. Scared.

"Don't be worried," I told her. "Why is she worried?" I asked Tristen.

He blinked, then turned back to Bliss. "He'll be here in a minute. Why didn't you call me?"

A long pause.

"I knew she was getting sick. It's my fault," Tristen muttered.

"A lot of things are your fault."

"No …" I croaked out. "Don't yell at my Tristen." I pulled the covers closer to me and coughed. "My throat hurts."

God, that was obvious. I giggled.

Hands grabbed at my blankets.

"No, mine!" I shouted, but it came out in a mere whisper. My arms were too heavy and weak to fight for my comforter.

"She's delirious," Bliss said harshly.

Shoulders under my arms. Two guys.

One was Tony.

"I remember you! You and Bliss are in love."

Tony grunted.

I swiveled my head the other way. Tristen.

"You're too close to me," I told him.

His shoulders tensed.

"But not, like, physically," I assured him.

His shoulders did not relax.

"Jesus, Kenz. Now isn't the time to get philosophical." Bliss's voice sounded from behind me.

It was too hard to stay awake. I couldn't do it.

"Good night," I told Bliss dreamily.

"She's going to pass out!"

Too late.

20

RECOVERY

I was hot. Too hot. There was a body pressed against mine in bed. Why was there someone in my bed?

My heart lurched.

Tristen.

But when I peeled my eyes open, it was a pale, feminine face I saw, dark circles under her eyes. Not Tristen. Bliss.

Wait, Bliss was in bed with me? The beeping of machines and a stringent hospital smell assaulted me all at once. Fuck, I was in the hospital.

Shaking, I reached out to touch Bliss's hand.

Her eyes flew open. "Oh my God. You're awake!" she croaked. She fished for the cord on the bed and pressed a button.

"Don't be dramatic." My voice was scratchy.

"You scared the shit out of us. You don't get to tell me not to be dramatic." She pulled her hair back into a low ponytail.

"Us?"

Bliss gave me a death stare as a nurse hurried in the room.

"She woke up!" Bliss told her. "For real this time."

The nurse shoved a thermometer in my mouth, talking in a soothing tone, but I couldn't concentrate on anything she said. All I saw was my poor best friend, her clothes wrinkled, her eyes dry and scared as she looked at me.

"I love you," she told me. "Don't *ever* do that again."

I leveled a sarcastic look at her, but I didn't try to talk again.

She laughed because she knew what I meant. It wasn't my fault I'd gotten sick.

"The nurse said you must have let it go a while for your pneumonia to get to this point," she accused.

I lifted my free shoulder. My other arm sported a blood pressure cuff and an IV.

I had been off for a bit. Cold. Tired. But the intensity of Maple House had surpassed all that. My standoff with Tristen must've made me fall apart in more ways than one.

Bliss studied my face. "What the hell happened?"

"Tristen is …" My voice gave out.

She whipped out her cell phone, opened a Notes app, and forked it over.

My thumbs flew as the nurse tsked us, still trying to check me over.

Tristen is one of the guys at the sex house.

I handed her the phone, and her eyes widened.

"Let's let her finish," she said, nodding meaningfully at the nurse.

When the poor woman finally left the room, Bliss was all over me.

"Holy shit, Kenz! Holy shit! Did you sleep with him?" She perched on the edge of the bed.

I shook my head.

"Who would have thought …" She trailed off when she saw my face fall. "It makes sense now."

"What does?" I whispered.

"What you were saying in your sleep."

What the hell did I say in my sleep?

"It wasn't that bad, I swear, but you might have said that you loved *your* Tristen. That you wanted *your* Tristen. But, Kenz, you can't have it both ways. You can't spend a week humping guys, then turn around and judge him for wanting sex like you did."

But it wasn't the same at all. He would continue to sleep with people, like, all the time. We wouldn't be exclusive, and despite the confidence Maple House had taught me, I still wanted that with him. And I couldn't have it.

I lay back against the pillow and closed my eyes. "Tired," I rasped, and it was true, but it was also true that I wanted to shut out this entire mess. It wasn't a real solution, but it was the temporary one I needed.

When my eyes flicked open again, Tristen was sleeping in a chair pulled up right next to my bed. I moved to sit up, trying frantically to smooth what I knew had to be the worst hair day ever. When the tube pulled and the scratchy bedding made a rustling noise, I froze. I didn't actually want to wake him up. I was too weak for the conversation I knew was coming. The one that would end things for good. Maybe I would always be too weak for it.

Instead, I watched the way his chest rose and fell, his breathing so even and deep. My eyes traced the curve of his neck as his chin rested on his chest. I skimmed over his relaxed face, centering on the dark shadows of his thick eyelashes.

Then I said my final good-bye. Good-bye, everything perfect and beautiful and amazing.

I'd miss the way he genuinely listened hard to everything I said and provided comfort without pumping me for information.

I could live a thousand years and never deserve him, but he didn't deserve me either.

His eyes flipped open, and I pretended to sleep until my body relaxed and performed the action for real.

I checked out of the hospital only hours later. When Tony came to pick us up, I studiously avoided Tristen's eyes as I took the front seat and he and Bliss slipped into the back.

"So, don't get mad …" she started.

I laid my head against the cool window. "What?" I might have just gotten the most sleep ever, but I was tired in a way I'd never been before, and my chest still hitched with every breath I took.

"You need to call Nan. They had to call her for permission to treat you since you were passed out and everything, so I told her what was going on, and …"

"Great." I fished my phone out of my pocket and dialed my mom.

She picked up on the second ring. "Oh, thank heaven. Are you okay? Bliss told me not to come out, but you know your father was already in the car, and I had to talk that man down."

"It's just pneumonia, Mom."

"You sound terrible. Do you know how many people die of pneumonia every year? What prescriptions did they give you? Have you filled them yet?"

Bliss snorted from the backseat.

I turned to give her a death glare and caught Tristen smiling, too. "The good ones. Yes, they're filled. I'm on my way back to the dorm to rest."

195

"Okay, well, I want you to call or text me every day. Sometimes, those prescriptions don't work, and you have to go back. Are you sure you don't want your father to drive down there and get you? You'd be more comfortable at home, sweetheart. Then I could look after you."

I gripped the phone. It was so tempting—to run away from what I'd done. To run away from Tristen; and even from Bliss, who knew too much; and Tony, who probably knew everything by now, too.

"No, Mom. I've got it. I just need to rest a little. I'll be fine."

"Fine," she conceded. "But no overdoing it. Have Bliss get your homework from your professors this week and bring it to you. I don't want you passing out again. You need your rest."

I turned to Bliss. She nodded.

"I love you, Mom."

"I love you, too, honey. So much."

I blinked back tears as we hung up.

The car was silent.

I cleared my throat. "I'm sorry for worrying you guys and for exposing you all. I hope you don't get sick."

"We'd be sick already," Tony said. "No worries."

"Worry is an understatement," Bliss grumbled.

Tristen elbowed her.

"Ow! What?"

We slowed to a stop for a crossing train, and Tony made eye contact with Bliss. After a second, he smiled that way boyfriends smiled at their girlfriends.

A hazy memory trickled into the back of my mind. *Did I say they loved each other? She's going to kill me!*

"Everyone gets sick," Tony said to me with a kind smile. "We have your back."

I snuggled into my coat and closed my eyes. The twisted feeling in my stomach had nothing to do with being sick and everything to do with the fact that Tony and Bliss were obviously together now. It had worked out even if I was a rat to say what I had, sick or not.

I wanted that with Tristen, but I couldn't even look at him.

"I'm sorry," I said the second we shut the boys out of our room.

"For?" She guided me to the futon and helped me take off my coat.

"I told Tony you liked him!" Well, kind of. I said they were in love.

She snorted. "I know."

"I'm a worm. I'm worse than a worm. I'm a flea on a worm."

"Worms don't have fleas, I don't think. It's fine, Kenz. It was the push he needed." She pulled my meds out of the bag, shook out a pill, and handed it to me.

"So, he asked you out?"

"Yep." Her expression remained neutral. She was deliberately hiding details from me as punishment.

"And you said …"

"I said yes. Then we made out in the corner of your hospital room. Happy?"

"Kind of, yeah. You like him!"

She sat next to me with a glass of water and smiled. "I really do."

I threw back the pill. "Let's celebrate."

"Let's get you to bed."

I wanted to protest, but my eyes were already closing. "For a celebratory nap."

She laughed.

When I woke up, I set myself a regimen of meds and studying. An hour of doing homework for each class, followed by a nap every day. I didn't work out at all, not that I'd ever been super into that. I forced myself to eat, but everything tasted like sawdust. I signed up for a dating app, only to delete it an hour into swiping left on everyone who wasn't Tristen. Copies of the Economics notes were slipped under our door, and I tried to pretend it didn't matter that he was still trying to take care of me.

After almost a week of my being MIA, things returned mostly to normal. I'd lost a bunch of weight, and staring at myself in the mirror was something I avoided. Not because my cheeks were thinner, but because my eyes were dead. And it had nothing to do with my brush with pneumonia.

Tristen and I were obliterated. I had accepted it even if he was still being polite. My body was just taking longer to get on board.

I dragged my ass to Economics on Monday, where the professor made a point of waving to me. I was pretty sure he hadn't even known I existed before, but someone had obviously told him I'd gotten sick. I scrunched into myself as I sat in the middle. It was the only safe space I could find—right between Brayan in the front, who no longer even registered on my radar, and Tristen, whose eyes bored holes in the back of my hoodie.

Tristen, who caught me right outside the door and kept a slow pace with me as I trekked across campus.

"How are you feeling?" he asked. "You look …"

I knew I looked like shit. I rolled my eyes. "Thanks."

"Do you want me to help you back to the dorm?"

I flashed back to him supporting me as he and Tony had carried me to the car, then into the hospital. A rock settled low in my stomach.

"Thank you for everything you did when I was sick," I said stiffly. "Will you thank Tony for me, too?"

He nodded at the sidewalk, then cleared his throat.

"Can we start over?" His voice was steady, but his body language was aloof, his hands shoved in the pockets of his coat.

"I don't think that's possible." I blew out a slow breath in front of me, watching the steam before it disappeared in the winter cold.

"Well, shit." His voice was soft.

"Yeah, shit," I agreed. "But … I like you," I said. "And if there were no Maple House …" I stopped talking. There was no point in wishing for things that couldn't happen.

"I know. Who was in your last room?" he asked, his voice tight.

"Do you really want to know?"

"No." He squinted at the bright snow on the corner.

"It was Brayan." I couldn't resist telling him.

He was so closed off. Part of me wanted to hurt him, and part of me … part of me was tired of all the things we'd hidden. I wanted to lay it all out there. Let it play out. I could see the end of this conversation already. Our pieces could only move toward the end of the game now, and no one would win.

His eyes squeezed shut.

"It's over between me and Brayan."

He had to know that. It was the entire point of the house, wasn't it?

"I didn't sleep with him. I passed the test."

"You passed," he said, his voice neutral, but I knew I was supposed to treat it like a question.

"I passed," I repeated. My feet scuffed over the wet snow.

He toed the ground, gouging a hole in the freshly fallen snow. "I think I had you up on a pedestal. Like … I thought you were this great person."

"Thanks a lot." I flopped onto a nearby bench. It was coated in a thin layer of white, but I didn't bother to brush it off. I was too tired.

He sat down, too, then turned to face me. "I'm not saying this right."

No kidding. This was quite possibly the most cringe-worthy conversation I'd ever had.

"What I meant was, now that we're both so obviously human, can we just call it even?" He tried to smile but failed.

"Do you get paid?" I blurted out. "For being in the … house?"

I didn't know why this meant so much to me, but it did. The details of how he had come to be there, how the rooms worked, how many people frequented it … none of that mattered but this.

"It wasn't like that."

"Then what's it like?" I asked. "Everything this week has been all about me, but what about you, Tristen? How did you—why did you—I don't even know what to ask."

"And I'm not supposed to tell, but I don't know if that applies to you or—" He mouthed the word *fuck*. "No. I was never paid. No one is. We were told it was for … you. The selected girls. To help you gain confidence, but I … I don't know. I stopped believing that, I guess."

"Okay." I leaned forward until I was on my feet and started walking again. I didn't want to hear any more after all.

"Okay?" he asked, his voice betraying his shock that I wasn't going to push the issue as he followed me.

"I mean …" I didn't know what I meant. I held my hands out, helpless. "I don't know what else to say."

"I quit," he said, rushing to catch up with me. "I couldn't leave you in that hospital to go back to that room. I wanted to get out before, but I was too—"

"Horny?"

He blushed, which was just about the cutest thing he could've done. Damn his cute blushing.

"Something like that."

We walked back to our rooms, the silence between us filled with all the things he couldn't say, things that I didn't want to know anyway. It wouldn't change anything.

The next morning, I felt like me for the first time since before the mess that was this past week. My appetite was back, and the ten hours of sleep I had forced myself to get actually made me feel rested. My breathing was normal, and it was like nothing had happened.

And Tristen …

Had I dreamed it, or had we finally ended it?

I sighed over my poached eggs in the dining commons.

"Oh my God, just have sex with him already," Bliss said. "I'm tired of watching both of you mope around like someone killed your dog."

My head whipped around. God, she was loud.

"Shut up!" I hissed at her. "He might be in here!"

"So what?"

"Talking about me?" Tristen said, sliding his tray next to Bliss's to sit across from me.

I guess we were on speaking terms after all. Joking terms even.

But it wasn't exactly funny yet.

Bliss turned sideways to confront him, but it didn't deter Tristen. He'd always been so good with her.

Is his confidence an effect of the house? How did he get into something like that? And why did he leave? Was it because he was no longer passionate about their creed, or was it—

Stop. You said you didn't want to know.

"Actually, yes. We were talking about you. What do you have to say to that?" Bliss pointed at him with her fork.

"Bliss …" I said, a warning in my voice.

Tristen's eyes flicked to mine, assessing the situation. Then he winked at me.

What did that *mean?*

"Okay then, what were you saying?" He shoved a piece of bacon in his mouth.

I couldn't take him seriously when he did something like that. It totally ruined the sex-god image.

"I was telling Kenz that she should just sleep with you and be done with it."

A clump of egg got stuck in my throat, and I sputtered, groping for my water glass. Once I gulped down half the glass and was under control again, the shame set in. My face blazed red as I stared down at the eggs. Today was definitely a smoothie morning. Or a French toast morning. I took another drink of my water as Tristen and Bliss stared at me.

"Ignore her," I rasped.

"Maybe she has a point," Tristen said, his voice nonchalant.

My eyes whipped up to him, but he was gathering his tray. How had he eaten all his food so fast? He'd been here for maybe ten seconds!

He stood and met my gaze head-on. "But I don't want to be 'done with it' when we're through. Not by a long shot. Ball's in your court, Kenzie."

And then he was gone.

Eyes wide, I turned to Bliss, who was chuckling over her spinach omelet.

"Why couldn't you leave it alone?" I hissed.

"Oh, calm down," she said.

Rage welled within me. "No. You have no boundaries!"

"It's going to help you in the end," she mumbled. "I'm giving you a push."

I wasn't buying it. "I don't need a push. You're not the puppet master of my life. You're supposed to be my friend!"

She grabbed my arm across the table. "I'm sorry."

I pulled away and covered my face with my hands.

"I really think there's something there, but you're right. It wasn't my place. Please don't be mad at me."

She never had a thought without saying it aloud. This we both knew. I couldn't hate my best friend for trying to help. I just …

"What do I do now?"

"Maybe talk to him?"

But we had talked. It didn't fix anything.

"And maybe listen this time?"

I sighed and got up from the table.

"You go, girl!" she called as I walked out of the cafeteria.

I waved over my shoulder.

Fuckin' Bliss.

21

OPEN YOUR EYES

I didn't care that I was supposed to be in class in five minutes. I also didn't care that I was playing into both of their hands. I stomped over to Tristen's door and slammed my fist against it over and over. Time to give him a piece of my mind.

When the door opened, Tony took a look at my face and said, "Er, hey. I'll just go hang out with Bliss."

"She's in the dining commons," I said sweetly.

"It's for you!" he called to Tristen as I slid past him, my chest heaving. Tony left, shutting the door behind him.

Tristen emerged from his room.

"You don't know!" I pointed my finger at him. "You don't know me! Neither of you do! I'm not going to let you trick me into having sex with you."

"You're right," he said, his hands outstretched in a helpless gesture.

"I'm—what?" My breath hitched as I stared up at him. "Stop that."

"Stop what? I'm sorry. You're right. You obviously don't have to sleep with me."

"Well, good." This wasn't how I thought this was going to go. "But I—"

"You what, Kenzie?"

He grinned broadly, not even bothering to hide how amused he was.

Bastard.

"Stop that. This isn't funny."

"Wanna watch our show?"

"No."

He wouldn't distract me by being all sweet and calling it *our* show.

"Then what?"

I stared at him, trying to muster up the anger I knew I should have at how high-handed he and Bliss were. But I couldn't.

I licked my lips, feeling completely out of my depth. Nervous.

His eyes followed the motion. He arched an eyebrow.

Was I brave enough to do this?

I nodded.

That was all it took. He pulled his shirt over his head, exposing a set of abs so glorious that I had to shut my eyes. I'd seen them in Maple House, but I'd been distracted by the situation then.

"Are you sure?" he asked, and this time, his voice was closer to me.

"Yes," I whispered.

I needed to know if he was different. If this would be different than the way I'd felt in The Hall of Art and Pleasure.

Then he bent down and kissed me. It was gentle, probing. A kiss that said, *I know you. I want you to feel safe.*

Tears gathered in my eyes. He was so incredibly sweet.

So, I kissed him back. But I couldn't be gentle like him. I gave him all the frustration of these past weeks, all my anger over what had happened between us. I bit his lip, and he groaned, his fingers digging into my hips, holding me against his body.

He pulled back, kneading my lower back under my hoodie. "Don't rush it," he said. "God, the way you kiss …"

I nipped at his neck.

"Hey now." He laughed.

His hands played with the hem of my sweatshirt, and I raised my hands.

I wiggled a little as he pulled it over my head. It hit the floor.

His eyes burned into mine as he dropped to his knees to slowly peel my sweatpants off, his mouth trailing hot kisses as he exposed each inch of skin.

And every movement, every touch was so Tristen. Tristen, who walked with me in the cold. Tristen, who watched my crazy stunts and supported me, even when I was dumb. Tristen, whose neat scrawl blended with mine in my math notes. Tristen, whose touch set me on fire. Who made me nervous.

My plain white push-up bra and panties were all that covered me now.

When he stood again, he leaned forward to caress my cheek. "You're not wearing makeup today."

I shrugged. "It's not me."

"I know who you are," he whispered.

"I know."

He led me over to the futon that he tipped back into a bed. Then he laid me down and stood above me, watching the way my chest rose and fell with wanting him.

"Come here."

What was he waiting for?

Beneath his gray sweatpants, he was rock hard, but he didn't drop them. He bent over, and his arms wrapped me in a hug as he undid the clasp of my bra. He tossed it off the futon like it offended him.

I couldn't help but giggle.

He turned back to me, a hungry expression on his face.

I drew in a breath as he descended to capture one of my nipples in his hot mouth. He swirled his tongue once, twice, three times around the hardening peak. I sank into his embrace, my breath hitching. I could hardly believe we were finally doing this, that I could feel this way, every moment heightened by the pain and pleasure of knowing him.

Without warning, he sucked hard, his teeth grazing the sensitive tip of my nipple.

I moaned, feeling the pull in the pit of my stomach.

He smiled against my skin, then fastened his mouth to my other breast, giving it the same attention as his hands massaged the outsides of my thighs. His mouth made its way from my chest down, kissing and nibbling. When he got to my inner thighs, I squirmed, my body hot and aching.

He raised his head, mischief in his glance. Then he skipped my most sensitive place, planting a hard kiss on the side of my stomach. I bucked against him.

"Kenzie."

The featherlight touch of his lips returned to the spot, driving me crazy and leaving me a whimpering mess. I was so turned on that I couldn't think straight.

"Please, please," I begged.

Slowly, he pulled down the soaked fabric of my underwear. He bent over me and took my right nipple into his mouth as his hand returned to my side.

I almost screamed at the sensation. How could I already be so close when he hadn't even touched me there yet?

"Tristen, I—"

He raised his head, looking at me. "This is how it should be," he murmured, his voice low and scratchy. "With someone who cares about you."

His hand moved down until he slipped a finger inside my heat and curled it forward.

Crying out his name, I clutched him to me, my fingernails digging into the muscles of his back.

"I love it when you say my name," he growled.

He hugged me close for a brief second before pulling away. My hands groped for him, and he caught one of them, holding on to me as he moved down, his chest brushing mine.

His mouth invaded me, hot and insistent as he threaded his fingers through mine. My clit was deliciously assaulted, and when he hit that sweet spot, my hips came up off the bed, bringing his face even deeper into me.

"Mmm," he moaned, pressing me back down. "You taste so good. My Kenzie."

My face heated. *His* Kenzie. I squeezed his hand with mine in the low light of the solitary lamp, and there was nothing to be heard but our breathing, my moaning.

His hand that had been holding me in place dipped in, and he pushed two fingers inside me as his mouth continued its onslaught. He thrust and twisted and licked. It was like he knew exactly how to touch me to drive me insane.

I lost my mind, squirming on the futon.

He moaned against me, the vibration adding a new sensation. I shut my eyes, my body shaking.

He pulled away, his fingers pausing inside me. "Open your eyes," he ordered.

I didn't want him to stop. My eyes snapped open and met his over the length of my body.

"I want to see," he said. "And I want you to watch me. I need it …" His eyes were fierce as he curled his fingers again. "I need it to be different … than the hall."

My breath caught. He wanted us to be different, too.

His head dipped back down, staring at me with his moody gray eyes, half-closed in the pleasure he was so obviously receiving from giving this moment to me. It was the most intimate thing I'd ever experienced.

It took effort to keep my head up in this position, but I couldn't have moved if the world had ended. It was such a turn-on, watching him bring back the pleasure, the urgency that, just a moment ago, I had thought I'd lost. Our eyes locked as he watched me moan, adjusting his fingers and his mouth to the places that rocked me most.

The muscles in my thighs tightened. I couldn't take it. I had to …

He pulled my hand that he was still holding sharply down, bringing his tongue deep inside me. The shock of it, the pressure … I was lost. I yelled out as I came hard, ripples of ecstasy running through my body. I wasn't in control of the noises I made as the tide of pleasure washed over me.

After what seemed like a lifetime, I started to come down. The waves were further apart, less strong. Tristen laid his cheek against the inside of my thigh, never breaking eye contact. And in those eyes were … everything.

When I was finally through, my body relaxed from its clenched state, though my head still reeled.

"Kenzie," he whispered as he touched me again with gentle fingers.

At this point, I was so sensitive that I almost cried out. I couldn't even think about doing more after that shattering orgasm. And yet … I needed him. My body throbbed with it. I grabbed a handful of his hair and yanked him toward me.

"Please, Tristen," I whispered, and he smirked.

Then he stood, and in one movement, he pulled off his clothes. I barely had time to take in his impressive erection before he disappeared behind the door of his bedroom. In the silence of his absence, I became acutely aware of what we'd just done, how naked I was, how exposed we'd be if Tony came back now and opened the door. I wished for a blanket, my clothes, anything. I folded into myself, trying to cover what I could. When he walked back into the room, however, his dick was sheathed in a condom.

"Don't," he ordered when he saw me. "Don't get shy now."

I opened my arms to him, though shy was exactly how I felt when I thought about his mouth on me. He sank down on top of me, kissing my neck as if he had all the time in the world, and after a moment, I relaxed into it, the heat of his skin permeating mine. Soon, I was impatient, all thoughts of modesty melting away. I needed everything. I needed him.

And he was so hard against me.

"Tristen," I implored.

He positioned himself, sinking into me inch by torturous inch. This was so right. I couldn't look away from his eyes as we connected as deeply as two people could. Those eyes saw everything—how much I wanted him, how wrecked our distance had made me. They accepted me, appreciated me, burned for only me in this moment. Who cared about Maple House? This was us.

When he started to move, the pace was agonizingly slow.

I couldn't take it. I arched up to meet him, and he groaned, squeezing his eyes shut.

When I repeated the gesture a second time, it was harder. "I need …"

Something in him seemed to break. He ground into me without warning.

I gasped in delight. Then it was all bets off, his hand pulling my thigh up to hitch my leg around his hip, both of us fighting to get closer, deeper, faster, harder.

I surrendered any control I had left, and we began to fight for the next orgasm.

I scratched at his back, grabbed his ass, and finally screamed into his shoulder as I came for the second time, my body sweaty and shaking. It was enough to push him over the edge as he slammed into me, shuddering against my skin.

We lay there for a minute, breathing in tandem, holding each other close, unwilling to break the connection.

Eventually, he pulled back and kissed the tip of my nose. "Earth-shattering," he said.

I had to agree. It had been … everything. Everything I had been missing. And it didn't have to be as crazy as any of the scenarios at Maple House. Our position had been completely basic. But it was different. More. Exactly as he had promised.

After a moment, a draft blew over us. I was totally naked. When would Tony be back? We hadn't even made it to Tristen's bed.

"Don't do that," he said, nuzzling my shoulder. "I can feel you tensing. Freaking out."

I nodded and pushed my hand through his hair, massaging his scalp. For once, I wouldn't overthink it. But I knew, deep down, that I'd been half in love with him before we began. And now … it was so complete—his possession of me—so scary.

"You're overthinking it right now, aren't you?" he asked, moving to brace himself above me.

I was trapped in the cage of his arms. Trapped in what I now felt for him. Would he throw me out now, be another Brayan?

"Breathe," he said gently. "Do you feel the same way as you did in," he faltered, "the house?"

I shook my head, and a smile fought its way across his face.

"Neither do I," he said. "But how do you feel?"

"Content," I said before I could censor myself.

He raised an eyebrow. "And …"

He waited.

"Attached. To you."

He pulled me close, our naked bodies meshing together in the tightness of his bear hug. "I'm attached to you, too."

My bruised heart stuttered to life.

"Am I your Tristen again?"

I shook my head against him. "No," I said.

My Tristen was innocent. But that wasn't the truth. The truth was, we were both allowed to be human. That was the way it always should have been.

"You're something better."

His arms released me, and he pulled me up to sit next to him. He nudged my shoulder with his, and I pushed him back, giggling.

"It's stupid and corny to ask this right now, but …" He trailed off, frowning.

This time, it was my turn to wait.

"Be my girlfriend?" He held his breath.

Everything had been building to this point.

"Yes."

ACKNOWLEDGMENTS

Writing is solitary, but polishing takes a village!

I want to thank my alpha readers for their diverse perspectives and my beta readers for their dedicated revision advice. I also want to thank The Odd Seed for giving me so many drafts of a cover that we both went cross-eyed and Jovana for her eye for detail.

I am so grateful for my family. Their unwavering support and sense of humor know no bounds.

Finally, a big thank you to my bestie, who never flinches before diving into the drastically different books I send. You're the real MVP.

CONNECT WITH DARCY

Thank you for reading *The Hall of Art and Pleasure*. If you enjoyed this book, please visit the site where you purchased it and write a brief review. Your feedback is important to me and will help other readers decide whether to read the book too!

And if you liked the first book in the Chasing Pleasure series...

Follow me to stay updated on upcoming books and events!

www.instagram.com/darcymonroeauthor

https://twitter.com/DarcyMonroeXXX

www.tiktok.com/@darcymonroexxx

www.facebook.com/DarcyMonroeAuthor

I'd love to hear from you!

Drop me a line anytime through my email:

DarcyMonroeAuthor@gmail.com

Or visit my website:

www.darcymonroewriter.wordpress.com

While you're there, sign up for my newsletter to get writing updates, exclusive bonus content, ARC opportunities, sneak peeks, and new release alerts!

www.ingramcontent.com/pod-product-compliance
Lightning Source LLC
Chambersburg PA
CBHW030312180626
46810CB00003B/1045